The US government wants to keep it secret...

An undercover CIA agent traveling with an archeological team stumbles upon a deposit of the strategic metal hafnium in the ruins of an Inca temple in the Andes mountains. Essential to manufacturing nuclear reactor control rods—it's every rogue state's dream come true.

While the US State Department rushes to negotiate for control of the mine, word leaks out, and jihadis and black marketeers develop competing plans to seize the mine and sell the hafnium to bad players around the globe.

National Defense Agency operatives KD Thorne and Jeffery Blunt track these criminal groups from the US to Europe to South America, where they uncover the details of the conspiracy. Will they find a way to turn the tables on these groups and keep them from taking over the mine? Or will KD, Blunt, and their allies die in the Andes at Agua Dulce?

The Hidden Mine at Agua Dulce is a careening rollercoaster ride that will keep you turning pages. If you like hard-to-figure-out plot twists and non-stop action, you'll love the fourth novel in the KD Thorne series.

THE HIDDEN MINE AT AGUA DULCE

A KD THORNE THRILLER

MICHAEL P. KING

BLURRED LINES PRESS

Blurred Lines Press

The Hidden Mine at Agua Dulce

Michael P. King

ISBN 978-1-952711-17-6

Cover design by Paramita Bhattacharjee at creativeparamita.com

The Hidden Mine at Aqua Dulce is a work of fiction. The names, characters, places, and events are products of the author's imagination or are used fictitiously. Any similarity to real persons or places is entirely coincidental.

For Sarah, all my love

1

Captain KD Thorne spotted Warrant Officer Jeffrey Blunt standing at the elevator in the lobby of the National Defense Agency building in Suitland, Maryland, as she passed through the security checkpoint. She caught up to him before the elevator opened.

"Blunt. Surprised you got here so fast with the traffic against you," she said. She pressed the third-floor button.

"Started earlier than you, Doc," Blunt replied.

"In a hurry to get away from your wife?"

"You know better than that. Almost called in sick."

"I'd like to see that. Skip out on a meeting with the assistant director."

"I said *almost*."

The elevator opened and they got off.

KD was five feet ten, with long, dark hair braided down her back and a thin scar crossing her left cheek. She'd served in Afghanistan before a tour at NASA had gone bad and she'd rebooted herself at the NDA. Blunt, six feet tall, a Black man who liked to fit in, was a SEAL team trained operator. They'd originally served together in Iraq.

"You know why she called us today?" Blunt asked. "We just got back. Supposed to get a week off."

"You getting old, Blunt? Need your beauty sleep?"

"Don't start this early in the morning, Doc."

KD knocked on the door and they went into the conference room. Clara Garcia, the assistant director of the NDA, sat on the other side of the table dressed in her usual black pantsuit, a silver cross dangling from her throat. Tina Han, a thirty-something Asian American who supervised the NDA's tech department, sat at the end of the table, her laptop computer in front of her, the tattoos on her wrists peeking out from under her shirt cuffs.

"Close the door and sit down," Garcia said.

KD and Blunt sat on the side of the table opposite Garcia.

"About six months ago," Garcia said, "an international archeological team found the ruins of an Inca temple in the mountains on the border between Chile and Bolivia."

Tina put a satellite photo of the site on the flatscreen TV mounted on the wall at the far end of the table. It showed an archeological site in a dry, mountainous area. She zoomed in. A small step pyramid, covered in grasses and shrubs, came into focus.

"That's an excellent picture," Blunt said.

"That's the new high-resolution satellite imaging," Garcia replied. "That's how the scientists found the place."

KD nodded.

"Inside these ruins they found a mine shaft. The locals dig out small amounts of zircon crystals that they use for ceremonial purposes. The geologist with the team thought the underlying ore looked unusual. So she brought back a sample and ran some tests. Turns out the ore contains a substantial amount of hafnium."

"Hafnium," KD said. "Why does that sound familiar?"

"It's a rare strategic metal used in the manufacture of nuclear reactor control rods."

"So we've got to have it," Blunt said.

"The only mineable deposit in the US is in California," Garcia said. "Most of the significant deposits are in countries that won't share it. So, yes, we've got to have it, and we've got to make sure rogue states don't get any of it. They can't build nuclear reactors without control rods, and they can't enrich nuclear fuel to make bombs without a reactor."

"What's the nationality of this geologist?" KD asked.

"CIA."

"So we were expecting to find the metal?" Blunt asked.

"Someone had reason to believe that we would find something," Garcia replied. "Hafnium tends to be found in certain kinds of silicate deposits near earthquake fault lines."

"Is the site in Chile or Bolivia?"

"That's an open question. Until now, there's never been a reason for either country to care."

"Where's the geologist now?" KD asked.

"She's down at the ruins, documenting the site, making friends with the locals at a tiny village next to the temple while the State Department is negotiating with Chile and Bolivia so that we get access to the ore no matter which country the mine is in. And we're coordinating with our allies, so we're all on the same page. In the meantime, as long as this is disputed territory, there's no local military or police."

"So why do you need us?"

"The CIA was hiding the hafnium sample at a Smithsonian lab. Last month, someone broke into the lab and stole the sample—or thought they did. They actually stole the wrong ore."

"But you're sure they were looking for the hafnium?" KD asked.

"The sample they took is unimportant."

"But this happened a month ago?"

"The stolen material was so unimportant that the FBI shelved the report."

Blunt cut in. "But the CIA found out anyway."

"Yeah. They moved the sample, and they want to know who's after it, but they can't act in the US. So it fell on our plate. No one is supposed to know about this new source of hafnium. This is a priority mission. Find out who's after it. Keep me updated."

Garcia left the room.

KD turned to Tina. "What have you got?"

"I've been digging into it. I did a full background on all the employees at the lab. One technician, Omar Kalish, has financial problems and family living in Poland. I'll email the file to your secure computer."

THAT AFTERNOON, KD and Blunt drove over to the materials processing lab at the Smithsonian Department of Mineral Sciences in Washington, DC. A supervisor in a lab coat met them at the entry. They showed their identification.

"How can I help you?"

"We need to speak with Omar Kalish," KD said.

"Is he in trouble?"

"Not at all. We just need his assistance."

"He's not at work today. Took a sick day."

"Thank you."

They walked back out to their Ford Explorer in the parking lot. Blunt got in the driver's side. "Try his house?"

"Might as well."

They drove north through Washington, DC, to Silver Spring, Maryland. Omar Kalish's house was a small, two-story on a street with children's bikes lying in the yards. They pulled to the curb in front of the house and walked up to the front door. A Toyota Camry was parked in the driveway. Blunt knocked on the door.

A middle-school-age girl came to the door, earbuds in her ears. "Yeah?"

"Is Omar Kalish at home?"

She turned into the room and yelled. "Dad!"

A few minutes later, a skinny, balding man dressed in pajamas came to the door. "Yeah?"

"Mr. Kalish?"

"Yes."

They showed their IDs. "I'm Agent Thorne and this is Agent Blunt. We're with the NDA."

"NDA? Never heard of that."

"Not many people have," KD continued. "We'd like to ask some questions."

"Come on in," Kalish said. "Let's go to the dining room. It's quieter there."

They passed through the living room, where two teenage boys were playing a shooter game on the TV, and sat down at the dining room table.

"How can I help you?"

"There was a robbery at your lab about a month ago," KD said.

"I heard about it, of course, but I don't know anything specific."

"Was there vandalism? What was taken?"

"I think the FBI investigated. I guess they wrote a report."

"But what did you see?"

"Someone broke in at night. Bypassed the alarms. Nancy—the boss's administrative assistant—called it in when she arrived in the morning. Nothing was disturbed as far as I could see when I got to work. I heard that they broke into a storage locker, took a mineral sample. Some sort of special iron collected from a mountain peak. The scientists involved were really angry. They won't be able to get back up on that mountain until next spring."

"What do you do at the lab?" Blunt asked.

"My group analyzes mineral samples."

"But you hadn't analyzed the special iron sample yet?"

"No."

"I understand you have family in Poland."

"I was born here. I'm an American citizen."

"Of course. But you have cousins in Poland?"

"Yes."

KD nodded. "Thank you for your time." She laid her business card on the table. "If you think of anything else, give us a call."

KD and Blunt walked back down the sidewalk to their SUV.

"He was wearing his jammies," Blunt said. "But he didn't look sick."

"No runny nose or cough. Didn't look pale or tired," KD added.

"Maybe he's all better."

"Maybe."

Blunt got in behind the wheel. KD took out her phone and called Tina Han. "Put a tap on Kalish's landline phone and gain control of his internet and computers."

"I'll have it done within the hour."

"Then when he's on the phone, put in a few clicks so that he'll think he's being tapped."

"You want him to know?"

"Yes." She ended the call.

Blunt chuckled. "Think the rabbit will run?"

"An innocent person thinks they're being tapped, they call us or call the police or convince themselves nothing is wrong. A guilty person, on the other hand—"

"Goes somewhere to make a call." Blunt pulled away from the curb. "Guess we're buying some take-out and coming back for the show. Where do you want to go? It's your turn to pick."

"In Silver Spring? What about the Parkway Deli? They make a good Reuben."

Blunt turned right at the corner. "I'm not sure how to get there. Can you find a route on your phone?"

KD opened the map app on her phone. "It's close. Take a left at the next traffic light."

LATER THAT EVENING, after the lights had gone out at Kalish's house, KD and Blunt watched Kalish quietly close the front door and get into the Camry in the driveway.

"Well, well, well," Blunt said.

"Might just need some more NyQuil," KD replied.

They followed Kalish to the nearest strip mall, where he pulled into a parking place in front of a twenty-four-hour drugstore. Blunt pulled into a spot in the parking lot with a good view of the front of the store. Kalish got out of the Camry and went inside.

"You're up," Blunt said.

KD took a GPS tracker out of the glove box, strolled across the parking lot to the Camry, bent down as if she'd dropped something, and placed the tracker under the bumper. Then she went into the drugstore. She spotted Kalish at the counter talking to the clerk and ducked down the nearest aisle. His back was to her. She watched him buy a cell phone. After he left the store, she called Tina. "Kalish just picked up a burner."

"Brand?"

KD stepped out of the aisle and looked at the cell phone display. "CallMore."

"Hold on." The line was quiet for a minute. "They use Sprint's towers. I'm going to use your and Blunt's phones to find the nearest cell tower."

KD ended the call and then called Blunt. "Is he gone?"

"Just left."

KD hurried out of the drugstore. "Let's go. I've got Tina trying to work her magic."

Blunt drove out of the parking lot. "Where to?"

KD looked at the GPS tracker signal on her map app. "He's on Sligo Avenue, headed away from his house. Go straight through the next intersection and take the next right."

They followed Kalish out Sligo Avenue and onto Valley Street and watched him pull over to the curb. An old panel van and a Ford Focus were the only other vehicles parked on the street. KD and Blunt drove by and parked around the corner on Mississippi Avenue.

KD called Tina. "Have you got his phone?"

"No. Too many cell phones using the tower."

"But you're out here at Sligo Park?"

"Yes. I'm just telling you, KD, it's a no go. He'd have to be on the phone at 3:00 a.m. for me to have a chance."

"Can you get a stingray device on him?"

"First thing in the morning, I'll have a team with a cell tower simulator at his house before he uses any of his cell phones the first time."

"Thanks, Tina." KD ended the call. She turned to Blunt. "You heard?"

"Yeah. It was worth a try, though."

"No reason to follow him anymore tonight. Let's go home."

THE NEXT MORNING, an electrical contracting van sat on the street across from Kalish's house. Inside, two NDA agents sat at the console of the stingray device—a cell tower simulator that attracted all the nearby cell phone transmissions and then routed them on to real cell towers. They sorted through the transmissions of all the nearby houses until they locked onto the Kalishes' phones. Then they eliminated the teenagers' phones. When Kalish finally used his phone—he was calling in sick again—they dropped a trojan horse into the weather app, and then unlocked a program so that they could use his phone as a recording device.

After an hour, it was clear that this was his usual phone, not the burner, so they recorded his conversations and waited for him to use the burner.

IN THE MEANTIME, KD and Blunt sat in their office at NDA headquarters rereading all the background information on the hafnium, the temple ruins, and what the CIA geologist Dr. Cora Rodriguez had learned about the villagers since she'd been there.

"Agua Dulce," KD said. "Sweet Water. A town too small to show up on a map."

"She's been busy," Blunt said.

"Helps that she's Latina, speaks Quechuan and Spanish—"

"And the science nerd cover doesn't hurt. Telling the villagers about the ore was genius. Makes her trustworthy."

"But now the villagers have split into two factions: the ones that want things left alone and the ones who want to mine the ore and get all the things the money can buy."

"Glad I don't have to sort that out," Blunt said.

"Yeah," KD replied. "And the clock is ticking. Somebody trying to steal the sample means that somebody knows about the ore."

Their landline phone rang. KD answered it and put it on speaker. "Yeah?"

"KD," Tina said. "Kalish left his house. The stingray is following him."

"Where is he headed?" Blunt asked.

"He's crossed into DC, headed down Sixteenth Street toward Rock Creek Park."

"We're on our way."

They took the elevator down to the basement parking garage, got in their Ford Explorer, Blunt driving, and sped out onto the Suitland Parkway, heading north toward DC.

"Think he'll make a call from the park?" Blunt said.

"That would be too easy."

"We deserve easy."

KD's smartphone buzzed. It was Tina. "What's up?"

"He's pulling into an urgent care clinic."

"Send me the address." The address popped up on her phone. She copied it to her map app. "Thanks, Tina."

She turned to Blunt. "You hear that?"

"Yeah. Just tell me where to go."

Twenty minutes later they pulled into the parking lot for Rock Creek Urgent Care. The electrician's van was parked near the exit. Kalish's Camry was parked near the front doors. KD called Tina. "We're here. Anything happening?"

"An operative followed him in. He went to the counter, filled out an intake form. He's sitting in the lobby waiting his turn to see a doctor. Can't hear anything in the room. Must have his phone off. The operative with the stingray is sorting out all the in-use phones."

"Okay. Kalish does anything, you call."

They sat in the Explorer, watching the front of the building. "Wish we could go inside," Blunt said.

"But we can't," KD replied.

Ten minutes later, Tina called. "Kalish has been called back to a treatment room."

"Okay."

"Hold on." The line was quiet for a minute. "He's using the burner."

"You sure? Can you record what he's saying?"

"Not yet."

"Where's the location he's talking to with the burner?"

"He's pinging off a cell tower in Arlington, Virginia."

"So we need a stingray on that tower."

"Wait. We're recording now."

"Anything?"

"We're starting in the middle of the conversation. Kalish says, '*I'm doing. I kept my promise. It's not my fault you screwed up. I need help.*' Other voice says, '*Stop acting guilty. Go back to work. You'll be fine. Stop calling me.*' Then Kalish hung up."

"But you're still recording?"

"No. Didn't have time to drop in a trojan horse, so we can only record when he's using the phone."

"Thanks, Tina." KD ended the call. She turned to Blunt. "Last time was good-cop, good-cop. This time it's bad-cop, bad-cop."

"About time."

They stood on the sidewalk in front of the urgent care clinic and waited for Kalish to come out. "How are you, Mr. Kalish?" Blunt asked.

Kalish glanced around. "How did you know I was here?"

"We've been following you, Mr. Kalish," KD said.

"What were you doing out by Sligo Park last night?" Blunt continued.

"That's none of your business."

"Either you're cheating on your wife, or that is some sorry trade-craft," Blunt said.

"Just like using the burner phone in the doctor's office," KD added.

"I don't have a burner phone, whatever that is."

"This is the twenty-first century, Mr. Kalish." KD snapped her fingers. "You do it. We know it."

They took Kalish by the arms and led him to their Explorer, where they put him in the back seat. They got into the front seats and locked the doors.

"Am I under arrest?" Kalish asked.

"We're not the police," KD replied.

"No," Blunt continued, "we're much worse."

"You can't hold me."

"We can do whatever we want," KD said. "You're going to answer our questions. You're going to tell the truth, or you're going on a one-way trip to an overseas black site."

"You can't do that. I'm an American citizen. I have rights."

"Terrorists have to earn their rights, Mr. Kalish."

"I'm not a terrorist."

"Whatever," Blunt said.

"Let's start at the beginning," KD continued. "Someone wanted to steal a particular ore sample from the mineral sciences lab. They came to you. You told them which locker. They screwed up."

"I don't know what you're talking about."

KD turned to Blunt. "Start the car."

"Where to?" Blunt asked.

"Joint Base Andrews."

"You can't do this," Kalish said.

"You must be confused, Mr. Kalish. We're not here to arrest you or read you your rights or take you to jail. You tell us what we want to know, and you get in your car and go back to your life. You don't tell us, and you never go home. So someone wanted to steal—"

"Yes."

"Why did they come to you?"

"I have gambling debts my wife doesn't know about."

"That's all?"

"A criminal cartel in Europe was threatening my cousins."

"In Poland?"

"Yep."

"So you had to help?"

"I had to help."

"And now you're afraid you'll be found out?"

"Yes."

"Who's the guy you were talking to on the phone?"

"I don't really know. I've only met him once."

"Describe him."

"Middle-age, white, dressed business casual, sort of Southern accent."

"And you called him from in the clinic?"

"Just now? Yeah. That's what he told me to do."

"What's his phone number?"

He showed them the number he'd input to call his contact. KD wrote it down.

"Did he pay off your gambling debts?"

"No."

"Did he get the gangsters to leave your cousins alone?"

"Yes."

KD unlocked the SUV doors. "Get out. If we need you, we'll be in touch."

"So I'm free to go?"

"That's what I said."

"You won't tell my boss?"

"No."

Kalish got out of the Explorer and trotted across the parking lot to his car.

KD called Tina and put her on speaker. "We've got the phone number for the mystery man in Arlington."

"Give it to me."

KD read the number.

"We'll have the stingray set up on him by tomorrow at the latest,"

Tina said. "As soon as we have his name and address, we'll turn his life inside out."

"Let's just hope he's using this phone for all his dirt," Blunt said.

"Now that we've got him," Tina replied, "it doesn't matter how many phones or email addresses he has."

2

When KD got back to her apartment that evening, her ex-husband Frank was sitting on the sofa with his feet on the coffee table and his laptop computer open on his lap. His red beard had a little gray in it, but he was still built like the rugby player she'd met in college. He glanced up at her standing in the front hall and closed his computer. "Hey, Katie," he said.

She smiled. "I didn't expect to see you."

He crossed the living room to her. They hugged and kissed. They were in the early stages of getting back together. Frank wanted to remarry, but KD wasn't sure about it yet. She loved him, she'd forgiven him for leaving her because she didn't want kids, but she was still hesitant. He lived in Florida, where he worked on NASA projects for an engineering firm. He stayed at her apartment when he came to DC for business.

"How long are you here?"

"Just overnight," he said. "I've got another meeting in the morning, and then I fly back to Florida in the afternoon."

"That's a shame. Why didn't you text me?"

"Wanted to surprise you."

"I'm surprised." She stepped out of her shoes. "And you would have been surprised if I hadn't come straight home from work."

"Took the chance."

"So you're leaving tomorrow?"

"Briefing the White House Office of Science and Technology on the new project, then I've got to go back."

She stepped up to him, put one hand on his chest, and leaned in to kiss him again. "Bed first and then out to dinner?"

"You're reading my mind."

FIRST THING THE NEXT MORNING, when KD got to the office, Blunt was already at his desk. "You're running late, Doc. Frank in town?"

"I left on time, just got stuck in traffic."

"Get a look in your email. Tina's been busy."

KD sat down at her desk, turned on her secure computer, and opened an email from Tina.

Your guy is a nonstop talker. Attached is the background info and the pertinent transcript summaries of his phone conversations.

KD opened the attachment.

Jerry Davis, forty-three years old, lobbyist for Americans for Freedom, a rightwing organization lobbying for an end to South American and African immigration. Their main financial support comes from gun manufacturers and agricultural chemical manufacturers.

She scanned through the transcript summaries. When she was done, she swiveled her chair toward Blunt's desk.

"So Davis in connected to an illegal group that's not Americans for Freedom."

"Looks like lobbying is his cover job," Blunt said.

"And this illegal group wants to help jihadis, so that the US and European public will get scared, and then the US and European governments will promote whites only immigration laws."

"So they must know something about the hafnium, enough so that they were trying to steal the ore sample to find out if it was the real deal and worth the trouble to find the mine and share the info with their jihadi group. Put the jihadis in the mix to use the hafnium to develop nuclear weapons."

"Almost too crazy to believe," KD said. "How many times have you gone through these transcripts?"

"Twice."

"I'm going to make another pass."

"Maybe the next set of transcripts will provide some actionable details."

THAT AFTERNOON, KD and Blunt got an email from Tina that Jerry Davis had a five o'clock meeting in the Theater District in Washington, DC., so they drove over to Arlington, Virginia, taking US highway 66 over the Potomac River, in hopes of getting a look inside Davis's apartment in a high-rise apartment building near the Rosslyn Metro stop.

"Nice neighborhood," KD said.

"Davis must be doing okay with his cover job." Blunt stopped their SUV in a towaway zone with a clear view of the front of Davis's building and kept the engine running. He gestured toward an electric contractor van parked in a handicap space. "That must be Tina's guy."

KD called Tina. "Has Davis left yet?"

"Not yet."

A few minutes later, Davis came out and walked toward the crosswalk.

"Just like his driver's license picture," Blunt said.

"Just another white, middle-age guy in a business suit. Perfect camouflage for DC."

Davis crossed the street and followed the crowd of people heading toward the Metro stop.

"So much for learning anything from his appearance," Blunt said. "You ready?"

"Let's do it."

They went into Davis's building, rode the elevator up to the tenth floor, and walked down the carpeted hallway to Davis's apartment. Blunt pressed the doorbell. No answer. He rapped on the door with his knuckles. All quiet. KD kept watch while he picked the lock. The apartment had an open floor plan, living room to the right and kitchen/dining area on the left. On the other side of the living room, a hall led to two bedrooms, one fitted out as a home office. A monitor and a docking station sat on the desk, but the laptop computer was not there. Nothing of interest in the desk drawers.

They took a careful look through the living room console and the kitchen cabinets, but there was nothing incriminating, not even a handgun.

They walked back out into the hall before they spoke.

"His apartment is too clean," Blunt said.

"Yeah, he definitely errs on the side of caution. Good thing he likes talking on the phone."

They were back over the river and into the DC rush-hour traffic when KD got a call from the NDA control center. "You were tracking Omar Kalish?"

"Yes."

"He's been in a pedestrian accident."

"Where?"

"Outside the Metro stop at Silver Spring."

"What hospital was he taken to?"

"Let me check." The line was quiet for a few minutes. "Agent Thorne? Sorry, Kalish was dead at the scene. Hit and run."

"Police still there?"

"Police and ambulance."

"What's the address?"

KD and Blunt raced across town, using their siren and lights to cut through the heavy traffic. They found the ambulance and one police car on a side street three blocks from the Metro stop and pulled in behind the police car. Two uniformed officers stood outside the police tape that marked the perimeter, while a plain-clothes detective stood hunched over a blood smear on the sidewalk.

KD and Blunt showed their IDs to one of the uniformed officers, who raised the police tape for them to crouch under. "Detective!"

The detective stood and turned. "I'm Agent Thorne and this is Agent Blunt. We're with the National Defense Agency."

The detective, a Black man wearing a porkpie hat, glanced from KD to Blunt. "How's this involve you?"

"Mr. Kalish was helping us with an investigation."

"Of what?"

"We're not at liberty to say."

Blunt continued. "Is Kalish dead?"

The detective nodded. "Probably didn't know what hit him. Walking down the sidewalk, blindsided from behind, driver smashed him into this tree." He pointed to a large oak just on the other side of the sidewalk. Bits of cloth were stuck to the bark.

"So they didn't even try to stop."

"Nope. See the skid marks." He pointed to parallel tire marks on the pavement. "They start way too late to slow the vehicle down in time."

"Any leads?" KD asked.

"You're looking at everything we got. Hoping that canvasing the nearby houses will produce a description of the vehicle. Have you got anything to share?"

"Nothing. We had no reason to believe that Mr. Kalish was in danger."

"You calling this a murder?"

"We're just generally suspicious until we've got reason not to be."

KD and Blunt went back to their SUV. "What do we know?" KD asked.

"He had gambling debts, but nobody murders you over gambling debts. Dead people can't pay."

"He called Davis. Was that enough? Or were they watching him? Do they know about us?"

Blunt shook his head. "Poor dumb bastard got in over his head. Those kids are going to be wailing at his house."

"It's sad business, for sure. Maybe it was just bad luck, but until we know better, we've got to keep digging."

KD called Tina. "Kalish is dead."

"How?"

"Hit and run. Maybe an accident. Maybe murder. Have you got anything new for us on Davis's phone?"

"Nothing yet."

"If he makes any mention of the killing, we want to know immediately."

"Will do."

MEANWHILE, in his backroom office in a café on a crowded street in Ciudad del Este, Paraguay, in the tri border area where Paraguay, Brazil, and Argentina meet, Commander Bashir of the New Islamic Caliphate sat with two subordinates, all three dressed in dark suits without neckties. Across the table from them sat two men connected to a Juarez drug cartel. All eyes were focused on a digital scale on the table in front of them. It displayed an open pouch of uncut diamonds.

Bashir looked up from the scale and nodded. "You'll find your product at the usual warehouse."

"When is the next shipment?"

"It will be on time. We've dealt with our export control problem in Lebanon."

"Excellent."

The drug traffickers left. Bashir closed the pouch and handed it to the man on his right. "Take these to the banker. Have him verify the value, exchange for cash, and wire the money to the Turkish account."

"Yes, Commander."

He turned to the remaining man, his second in command. "Saad, the Caliphate Council is getting anxious. Have you heard anything new from Gomez?"

"No, sir. He's still at Agua Dulce. The villagers haven't made up their minds about what to do about the ore, but he still thinks he can persuade them to partner with us."

"And you trust him?"

"Ever since he came to work for us in Iquique, he's been reliable."

"What's his story?"

"Fairly typical. He came to the city to find work, didn't have any luck, couldn't pay his rent, and his wife took up with another man. One of our couriers found him on the sidewalk, saw potential, groomed him. He's good at getting around the police because he's a native."

"He's not a Muslim?"

"No, but he's motivated by money, and his cousin is one of the elders. He has no reason to lie."

"And the American is still there, trying to convince the villagers to partner with her. We have to find a way to push her out without raising suspicion."

"When they choose us, she'll have no reason to stay."

"Do you think she'll leave on her own?"

"I'll see if Gomez can do something about her."

"Good. We need every advantage. Our contacts tell us that the Bolivians and Chileans are at loggerheads, but we might only have access to the mine for a few months if they work out their differences. And if the Americans make a deal with whichever country ends up controlling the mine, they'll move in and take over. Our opportunity will be lost. Time is running out. If we can't get the villagers' cooperation soon, we'll have to overrun the village and force them to tell us where the mine is."

"It would be better to come to an accommodation."

"It would. But we have to do whatever we must to realize Allah's plan."

THE NEXT DAY, KD and Blunt followed Davis when he left his building in Arlington and took the escalator down into the Rosslyn

Metro stop. Davis was dressed in a suit and tie and carrying a briefcase. Thirty minutes later, he got off at the Capitol South Metro stop with the usual mix of staffers in business wear and tourists in casual clothes. KD and Blunt followed him north of First Street SE past the Capitol to the Russell Senate Office Building, where he passed through security and disappeared down the hall.

KD and Blunt sat on the nearest bench. "It's going to be a long day," Blunt said.

"Maybe," KD replied. "It just depends on what his rhythm is."

"I hate this sitting around."

An hour and forty minutes later, Davis came out of the Russell Senate Office Building and walked back down First Street SE to the Cannon House Office Building on the other side of the US Capitol. KD and Blunt found another bench to sit on. Fifty minutes later, he reappeared and walked back to the Metro station, where he got on a train headed west. He got off at Rosslyn and headed back to his apartment building.

"Waste of time," Blunt said.

"Unless he gets on his burner," KD replied. "Let's get some lunch." They went into a deli and ordered sandwiches and coffee at the counter. After they sat at a table in the front window with a view of Davis's building, KD called Tina. "Anything?"

"No. Just normal business."

"Have you gotten Kalish's autopsy report?"

"Clean tox screen. Massive trauma consistent with a hit-and-run."

"Do the cops have any leads?"

"Nothing. No one looking out the window. And they haven't found the vehicle yet."

"Thanks, Tina."

KD filled in Blunt.

"So we've got a big zero," Blunt said. "We going to dog him all day?"

"Do we have a choice?"

Davis stayed in his apartment the rest of the day. After rush hour slowed down, KD and Blunt went to a parking garage for their SUV and started back toward NDA headquarters in Suitland, Blunt driving.

"Are we doing more of this tomorrow?" Blunt asked.

"We know he's a bad player," KD replied. "Something's got to give."

"Unless he knows we're on him."

KD glanced over her shoulder. "I think the gray Suburban is tailing us."

Blunt looked in his rearview mirror. "Let's find out."

Blunt took a right down the next off ramp, sped under an overpass, and took the first left, screeching through the turn. Then he drove slightly below the speed limit for three blocks, but the Suburban didn't reappear.

"Guess I was wrong," KD said.

At the next intersection, the Suburban crashed into the driver's side of the Explorer, pushing it through the intersection and into a power pole. The airbags boomed. Two men in tactical gear jumped out of the Suburban with submachine guns as KD and Blunt crawled out a shattered window on the passenger's side of the Explorer. The two men sprayed the Explorer with gunfire. KD and Blunt returned fire with their handguns. Blunt rolled onto his side and fired under the Explorer, catching one of the assailants in the leg. He fell onto his side. Blunt shot him in the head. The other man backed along the side of the Suburban, firing in bursts. KD popped around the back of the Explorer and put a row of bullets into the man's vest. He slipped and fell to the pavement. A Ram truck skidded to a stop behind the Suburban. The passenger's door flew open. "Come on," the driver yelled. The man scurried across the pavement and dove into the truck. It sped off with the door swinging.

KD turned to Blunt. "You okay?"

"Yeah. You?"

"Got some bits of glass in my hair. My shoulder's banged up."

"So you're good?"

She nodded.

They came around the wrecked SUV, their pistols trained on the man lying on the pavement. KD kicked his machine gun away. Blunt crouched and checked his pulse. "Dead."

KD called the control center. "We've been ambushed. SUV is totaled. Need assistance. Got one bad guy dead at the scene."

KD and Blunt waited in the shadows of the building across the street. Twenty minutes later, an ambulance, a tow truck, and a silver Highlander pulled up in the street. The Highlander's driver, a technician on Tina's staff, took a photo of the dead man's face and captured his fingerprints with a portable scanner. "Thorne and Blunt, you're with me."

He debriefed them on the way to NDA headquarters, where a medic examined them in the infirmary. "Either of you have a bad headache?"

They both shook their heads.

"Well, your pupils look fine, so probably no concussion." He turned to KD. "I'm going to put your right arm in a sling."

"Do I really need it?"

"Try the sling for a few days. That shoulder's probably going to be sore tomorrow. Wearing the sling will help it heal faster."

They went up to their office. When they turned on KD's computer, an email from Tina was already waiting for them.

The DOA is Chris Moore. Two terms in prison: first for drugs, second for guns. Associated with the White Riders prison gang. Should have his local address by tomorrow. We're searching surveillance cameras for images of the other guy and checking hospitals for gunshot wound victims.

AT 9:00 a.m. the next morning, KD and Blunt were standing on the sidewalk in front of a duplex in Tacoma Park with a warrant and a tactical team. The left-side driveway was empty and the grass needing mowing. The right-side driveway contained an old Nissan Sentra and the yard had children's toys strewn about.

KD studied the left-side duplex. "I'm guessing no one's at home."

She nodded to the tactical team leader, who gave the go ahead to his team. They kicked in the front door on the left side and rushed in.

A few minutes later, the team leader gave the all-clear. KD and Blunt went inside. Rent-to-own furniture, empty refrigerator, unmade bed. A shotgun on the shelf in the bedroom closet. "Pretty sad," Blunt said.

"Let's talk to the neighbor."

KD knocked on the right-side duplex door. A young woman wearing a brown restaurant server's uniform opened the door. KD and Blunt showed their IDs.

"Sorry about the disturbance," KD said.

"What's this all about?" the woman asked.

"What can you tell us about your neighbor?"

"Not the kind of guy you'd want to know. Scary looking. Tried to avoid him."

"Any friends?" Blunt asked.

"Sometimes I'd hear talking through the wall, but I never saw anyone."

"Thank you," KD said.

They said their goodbyes to the tactical team and got in their SUV. "So we're back to square one," Blunt said.

"Maybe Tina will find some useful surveillance footage," KD replied.

"How about if we pick up Davis and sweat him? He set those killers on us."

"We don't have any proof."

"Do we need proof? I'm not saying we rough him up. I'm just saying that if we put some pressure on him, maybe he'll make a mistake."

The GPS surveillance on Davis's cell phone indicated that he was in his apartment in Arlington. KD and Blunt drove southwest through Washington and over the bridge into Virginia, where they parked on the street behind the utility van that contained the stingray device.

KD banged on the back door of the van before she opened it. The technician, a young man wearing blue work clothes, looked up from a computer screen.

"Anything?"

"Nothing. Just normal work talk."

"Thanks."

KD and Blunt went into Davis's building and rode the elevator up. "How's your shoulder?"

"It's fine. Just a touch sore. I think the medic overreacted."

"But you're still wearing the sling."

"Overabundance of caution."

Blunt pressed the doorbell. Davis opened the door. KD and Blunt showed their IDs. "I'm Agent Thorne and this is Agent Blunt," KD said. "We'd like to ask you some questions."

"Ask away."

"Could we come in?"

"No."

"Do you have something to hide?"

"You two have been following me. I'm tired of being harassed by you deep state goons."

"Why do you think we've been following you?"

"Because I've got eyes. You think you're invisible?"

"Do you know Omar Kalish?"

"Never heard of him."

"You answered a phone call from him four days ago."

"Must have been a wrong number."

"Did you know he was dead?"

"Do you think that's a trick question? I said I never heard of him. Look, I've got nothing else to say to you. Next time you want to talk, make an appointment and we'll meet with my lawyer." He shut the door.

KD and Blunt started back down the hall.

"He definitely got Kalish killed," Blunt said.

"But we can't get him with any evidence we obtained off the stingray," KD replied. "No court order. We'll have to wait until the stingray leads us to something we can use."

.   .   .

MEANWHILE, Dr. Cora Rodriguez, CIA, made her way down the hill from her tin-roofed, mud-walled cabin to Agua Dulce, the village next to the Inca temple ruins, her rucksack on one shoulder. She was dark skinned, with curly hair, and wore a straw cowboy hat against the sun. The hillside was covered in small, spindly trees and calf-high dry weeds that brushed against her legs as she walked.

The village was shaped like a cross, with thatched-roofed, clay brick houses running down both sides of the dirt street and an abandoned church with an open plaza in front of it at the head of the cross. On the left side of the plaza, several benches were situated around a thatched-roofed communal well. Because there was no electricity, the villagers usually did their chores outside in the daylight. Up the wooded hill from the right cross street were the temple ruins. The archeologists never would have found them if she hadn't provided the latest CIA satellite images.

When Rodriguez had first come here to build relationships with the locals, they'd been suspicious of her and hadn't wanted her among them, violating their privacy. So they offered her the shack on the hill, which worked to her advantage, since their privacy was also her privacy. But now she was a fixture in the village—if not one of them, then at least a person who was not notable.

As she made her way onto the main street, she smiled and waved at Maria Sinchi, an elderly woman who was sitting at a loom teaching her granddaughter to weave. She waved back. Her husband, Tomas, was one of the village elders who were skeptical about mining the ore. Desecration of the temple, too much change, too many strangers. Fortunately, Rodriguez thought, she didn't have to convince everyone. Just enough to create a consensus for mining.

Up at the plaza she turned right on the cross street. In front of Roberto and Anna Cuzco's house, Anna, a woman in her twenties dressed in worn-out jeans and an untucked work shirt, sat on a blanket, sorting potatoes. A baby swaddled in a basket lay beside her and a toddler played with a stick nearby.

Rodriguez stopped and spoke in English. "Hey, Anna."

"Hey."

She squatted next to her. "How is your son?"

"No different. He still doesn't speak."

"Sometimes these developmental issues sort themselves out."

She shrugged. "I don't think so. There's something very wrong. He's so different from the other boys his age."

"What did the doctor say?"

"The doctor in the market town? Nothing. He just shook his head and told us to get on with our lives."

"I'll pray for you."

"Thank you."

"Where's Roberto?"

"Around back."

Rodriguez went around to the back of the house, where a twenty-something man was shoveling out a pig stye. She continued speaking in English. "Roberto, how are you?"

Roberto wiped his hand on his pants. "I'm well." They shook hands.

"Are you still having a village meeting tonight?"

"Yes. We'll continue our discussion about the mining. I think we're getting close to yes."

"I hope so."

"Money for solar panels so that we can have electricity and the internet—that's very convincing to people who've been out in the world."

"But they have to convince their relatives."

"It's happening. If not tonight, soon. You going up to the temple?"

She nodded. "Still documenting the antechamber."

Rodriguez continued down the cross street and followed the wide path at the end that went up through the woods. At the crest of the hill was the ruin of a small Incan temple. Behind it on the left, a series of huge rocks rose straight up to a prominent spot overlooking the village. Most of the temple was covered in short, weedy grasses, though the steps of the lower part of the pyramid were still visible. Rodriguez walked around the side to an entryway and stooped through the low doorway to the antechamber.

She turned on her flashlight. The walls of the antechamber were covered with carved murals that depicted some sort of activity involving humans and bird people. A stone table covered in glyphs sat in the middle of the room, and behind it was a tunnel large enough for two people to walk side by side without stooping.

She could still remember the excitement when the archeology team first entered the antechamber. Everyone was taking pictures and talking at once. And then when they went down the tunnel to the mine face and she saw the purple zircon crystals standing out against the surrounding ore, it had been hard for her not to blabber. But it all seemed so long ago now.

She turned on the solar-battery-powered archeology lights that were arranged around the room, turned off her flashlight, found her place on the left side wall mural, and started taking zoomed-in photos with a digital camera.

THE NEXT MORNING, in Suitland, Tina met KD and Blunt at their office. "Found your guy who got away on a surveillance camera at an intersection two blocks away. Ran him through our databases. He's connected to the Blaze Group, a criminal syndicate based in Berlin."

"What's his name?" Blunt asked.

"Patrick Colbert."

"Can we find out his whereabouts?" KD asked.

"The CIA is helping with that. They spotted him on a surveillance camera coming out of the Paris Charles de Gaulle Airport, and then got eyes on him at a train station after he crossed into Germany."

"Can they pick him up for us?"

"I doubt it. The Germans are still angry about the last rendition we pulled on them. He hasn't broken any laws in Germany. At least none that they know of."

"So I guess we're going to have to go to him. Can you coordinate with the CIA and get us on a military flight out of Joint Base Andrews?"

"I'll make the arrangements." Tina left the room.

KD slipped her right arm out of the sling and started writing notes on a legal pad. "So Davis is connected to Colbert, who's connected to Blaze, which must be the criminal group that was threatening Kalish's Polish cousins. And they want the jihadis to have the hafnium so they can stop immigration. It makes no sense."

Blunt shrugged. "Maybe it will make more sense when we have our hands on him."

LATER THAT NIGHT, black marketeer Alexei Lysenko was sitting in the back seat of a Mercedes Benz limousine, riding through the traffic in downtown Madrid. His encrypted phone rang. He glanced at the screen, recognized the number as his contact with the Blaze Group, and answered.

"Speaking," he said.

"You do business with the New Islamic Caliphate, don't you?"

"They're a very good customer."

"They're attempting to take control of a mine on the Chile Bolivia border."

"Are you talking about the mine at Agua Dolce?"

"Yes."

"I'm already helping them secure it."

"Which makes you the perfect person to double-cross them and secure it for us."

"That sounds like a way to get on the wrong side of a jihad."

"We're a much bigger customer than they are. We expect you to help us. Don't make us look elsewhere. You want to make money, you have to take risks."

"We don't yet know where the mine is."

"Then do what you have to do to find out. You partner with us, and as soon as we take control of the mine and start selling the ore, there will be plenty of money to go around."

"Until the Chileans and Bolivians reach an accord."

"That's going to take a while. Two of the negotiators work for us."

"So you've been planning on this for a while."

"As soon as we found out about the hafnium. We weren't going to miss out on a once in a lifetime opportunity."

"Do you care how I find out where the mine is and push the Caliphate out?"

"No. Just let us know when we can start mining."

The Blaze operative ended the call. Lysenko looked out his car window at the streetscape rushing by. So Blaze was in and the Caliphate was out. Why hadn't he heard back from his contact? He should have gotten to Agua Dulce by now.

THAT EVENING IN AGUA DULCE, the village men gathered on the plaza in front of the abandoned church to discuss village business. The rains had been good enough and at the right time, so most families would have a surplus of corn and potatoes. The alpacas and pigs were free of disease. And many women had woven cloth to sell in the market town down the mountain. The only serious concern was the temple and the ore.

Everyone agreed that archeologists and other scientists would continue to visit the temple, at least for the foreseeable future. And that was not a problem, as long as they were respectful. The issue was the ore, which was valuable, according to Senora Rodriguez. If there was mining, there would be jobs, and money for solar power, satellite internet, and maybe a school. But what would happen to their way of life? No one wanted crime and congestion and immoral behavior. They wanted their children to stay, instead of leaving to work in the cities, but they didn't want outsiders with their strange ways making their homes in the village.

Roberto and the few other men who'd been out in the world were very convincing when they talked about all the modern conveniences that could be brought to the village. And Tomas and his allies were convincing when they talked about all the trouble mining would bring—the need for a sheriff and a city hall and formal ways of settling disputes, like they had in the market towns. And none of this touched on the sacred nature of the ore. Would the spirits be offended? Mining or no mining? It still wasn't clear what the village should do.

After the meeting, Tomas and Gomez, Tomas's cousin, walked back to their clay brick houses in the fading light. "I told you," Gomez said. "The village is going to make a mistake."

"The village," Tomas said, "is going to do what it thinks is right. And if that's mining the ore, so be it."

"Then we need more options. A choice of who to work with. We shouldn't just accept the Americans. None of them can be trusted."

"Senora Rodriguez has always kept her word. She told us about how valuable the ore is, and she promised not to reveal the location of the mine. She's not doing any harm taking pictures of the temple."

"The Americans want the ore," Gomez replied. "How much longer do you think they will be patient?"

"They will have to abide with our decision."

"You've never been out of these mountains, Tomas. You don't know these strangers like I do. They always promise one thing and do another."

"She's given no indication that we can't trust her."

"If she doesn't like our decision, there will be trouble."

"We'll see."

"We should get the best deal. Maybe someone else will offer us better terms."

"Like who?"

"I know some people who will show more respect for our faith because they are guided by their own faith."

"You mean church people? You know we won't allow priests in the village. Not after the incident with Amaru's daughter."

"These are Muslims."

"Muslims? Where did you meet them?"

"When I was working at the eastern border of Bolivia."

"I thought you were working in Chile at Iquique."

"I was, originally. But then I met a friend who knew about work in Bolivia."

"A Muslim?"

"Exactly."

"How well do you know these people?"

"Enough to know that they keep their word."

"Maybe you're right. Maybe we should hear what they have to say. But first we have to decide if we're mining at all."

3

KD and Blunt crossed the tarmac of Ramstein Air Force Base in southeast Germany and got into a silver Volvo parked near the terminal. A middle-age blonde wearing a gray skirt suit sat in the driver's seat. KD got in the front passenger's seat; Blunt got in the back.

The blonde turned to shake hands with them both. "I'm Kathy Roland."

"I'm KD and this is Blunt."

"How was your flight?"

"Uneventful. Our target still in Munich?"

"In a rowhouse in a town outside the city. We've got three agents on him. He's not going anywhere."

"Appreciate the help."

"You bet. It'll take about four hours to get there, so you might as well relax."

KD and Blunt lay back in their seats and went to sleep. When KD woke, they were driving down a gravel road in the dark, farm fields flashing by in the headlights on both sides. She stretched, glanced in the back seat at Blunt, who was already awake, and turned to Roland. "Where are we?"

"A little outside Augsburg. Coming into town so that we end up behind the house we're set up in."

They parked on the cobblestone street behind a two-story rowhouse. Roland unlocked the back door and led them in through the kitchen and up the stairs to the front bedroom, where three men dressed like locals were monitoring the surveillance cameras that they'd set up to watch the rowhouse on the corner across the street.

The surveillance team glanced back at them when they entered the room. "Anything going on?" Roland asked.

"A couple of guys have come and gone. That's about it."

"Can we look at the feed?" KD asked.

"Pull up a chair," the man at the laptop computer said.

KD and Blunt sat down on either side of the man. "He got there this morning. You want to start at the beginning?"

"Sounds good," Blunt said.

The man located the beginning of the feed and ran it at triple speed. Several men and one woman came and went from the house.

"Stop there," Blunt said.

The man stopped the feed. "Back up to the last guy?" he asked.

"Yeah. I think I know him."

The man backed up the feed to show a redheaded man wearing a leather jacket.

Blunt pointed at the screen. "That's one of Lysenko's guys."

"Lysenko? The black marketeer? You sure?" KD asked.

"I'd remember that rat bastard anywhere. Shot two of my guys in Italy about six years ago."

"What was the job?"

"Buying explosives. It was all going great until it turned to mud. And we didn't get far enough up the food chain to pop Lysenko."

"Lysenko and Blaze Group. Black marketeers and a crime syndicate after the hafnium. That makes a lot more sense than Jihadis and immigration politics."

Blunt turned to Roland. "Can we grab these guys?"

"Not in Germany," Roland replied. "We're already way over the line with this unauthorized surveillance. So unless you're looking for something in particular, we need to bag this up before the local cops get wind of us."

KD cut in. "Can you provide our tech team with access to the live feed? Let them monitor from our offices?"

"Yeah, we can do that. Just don't step on anybody's toes."

KD gave the man at the laptop computer Tina Han's encrypted email address, and he set up a link to the live feed and emailed it to her.

"Thanks."

"Anything else?" Roland asked.

"I guess that's all we can do. We'll have to trail them at a distance."

"Back to Ramstein?"

"Yeah," KD said. "If we can't pick up Colbert or Lysenko's guy, there's nothing for us to do here."

After Roland dropped KD and Blunt off at the terminal at Ramstein Air Force Base, KD called Tina. "Are you on the surveillance feed?"

"Yeah. I put my best team on it. And we're tracking Lysenko's guy using the public surveillance cameras, so within a several hour window we'll know where he is, more or less."

"We're going to stay in Germany a few days. Once the CIA clears out, we'll make a try for Colbert."

"I'll let Garcia know."

PATRICK COLBERT SAT on the worn-out sofa in the safehouse, smoking a cigarette. People had been coming in and out like it was the waiting room of a doctor's office. He was sure he'd made a clean escape from the US. They'd handled the Kalish problem, and his partner on the botched job was dead, so he didn't know why he was waiting here for a phone call from his Blaze contact.

He put out his cigarette in a cup of cold coffee and went into the kitchen to get a beer from the refrigerator. Smith, the man who ran the safehouse, poked his head in the kitchen door. "We're ordering take-out. You want in?"

"Where from?"

"Chinese or pizza."

"Chinese. Moo shu pork, if they've got it."

Smith disappeared. Colbert felt the burner phone he'd been given that morning vibrate in his pocket. "Yeah, hello."

"Colbert?"

"Yes, Mr.—"

"No names. You know who's speaking?"

"Yes."

"Your last job went fifty-fifty."

"The partner your guy chose left much to be desired."

"Well, you're too hot for the US right now, so we'll just have to hope you warned them off."

"Fine by me."

"We're doing some work with Lysenko right now. There's a shipment coming into Madrid and going to Barcelona. We want you to ride shotgun."

"When do I get paid?"

"After this next job we'll settle up. Go to Lyon to the Magpie Cafe. Be there at four-thirty. Lysenko's guy will fill you in on the details." The line went dead.

Colbert put away his phone. Stalling on his payment—that wasn't like Blaze at all. And then hiring him out to Lysenko. What was that about?

He rubbed his shoulder. Flesh wound was healing nicely. Maybe Blaze was losing their touch. Chris Moore had been the bottom of the barrel—a racist gangster with no impulse control. The kind of guy who would spill his guts for a lighter sentence. If he hadn't died, he probably would have killed him to tie up loose ends. Well, he'd see this job through, but maybe it was becoming time to move on.

. . .

RODRIGUEZ'S EYES SNAPPED OPEN. Moonlight fell into her cabin through the partially open shutters in the far window. She could hear —what? A rat or some other creature moving across the floor, maybe? She shifted her head and peered into the blackness beyond the shaft of moonlight. For a second she thought she saw the sleeve of a coat. She blinked. Nothing. She strained her ears. Nothing. Maybe her mind was playing tricks on her. She rolled over.

The blow glanced off the side of her skull. She sprang up off the bed in a fighter's crouch, felt the movement of the air as something whooshed by a few inches to her right, and stepped forward as she punched hard into where her opponent should be, striking someone who fell backward. She grabbed the flashlight from her night table. A man dressed like a villager scrambled off the floor and ran out the door. She started after him but stopped in the yard. It would be crazy to run out in the dark in the middle of the night.

She went back into the cabin, turned on a camping lamp, and picked up her pistol from the shelf by the bed. She felt the side of her head. Her hand came away bloody.

She went to the mirror over the wash basin and held the camping lamp up near the side of her head. An inch-long gash ran down behind her ear. She got out her first aid kit, cleaned the wound, and taped it closed. She put the first aid kit away and sat on the edge of the bed. What did she see? It had happened so fast. It was definitely a man. Might have been a villager, but she couldn't be sure.

But why attack her now? She'd never felt any hostility from any of the villagers since she had been here. Sure, some were against mining, but their disagreements had always been respectful. Yesterday's village meeting had been inconclusive, although it was becoming clear that they would eventually decide to mine. Could it be someone foolish enough to think they could stop the mining if they scared her off? Or was there some other organization hoping to get the contract when the villagers finally made their decision? Who was well-connected enough to have a villager in their pocket ready to murder for them? She got out her satellite phone and called the CIA control desk.

"Code, please."

She input her code.

"Speak."

She explained what had happened.

"I'll relay this information to your supervisor."

She ended the call, locked the window shutters and the door to the cabin, and lay down on her cot with her pistol in her hand.

GOMEZ STOOD in the dark by a clump of tall bushes along the meandering foot path. "What happened?"

His cousin Alfredo looked back up the hill toward Rodriguez's cabin. "I thought I would stab her in her sleep, but she fought back."

"So?"

"I'm sure I drew blood, but she attacked me, knocked me down and turned on a flashlight. I didn't know she was a trained fighter."

Gomez put his hand on Alfredo's shoulder. "No worries, cousin."

"We've lost the element of surprise."

"But now she doesn't feel safe. Maybe she'll decide to leave. Go back to your house. Don't tell anyone."

Alfredo disappeared into the dark. Gomez took a satellite phone out of his rucksack. The phone rang six times before Saad came on the line.

"Speak."

"We tried to eliminate the American, but she escaped."

"Were you identified?"

"No."

"Have you made any progress with the villagers?"

"A little. As they come to accept that there will be mining, I'm trying to convince them that you would be a better partner than the American consortium."

"Keep watch on the American and keep trying to convince the elders."

"I will."

"If you're successful, we will double your fee."

· · ·

SAAD ENDED THE CALL. He set his satellite phone down on his bedside table, picked up his smartphone, and called Bashir.

"What is it?"

Saad went over his conversation with Gomez.

"You did the right thing calling me. Gomez's heart may be in the work, but he might be too incompetent to get the job done."

"Only time will tell."

"That's what I'm afraid of."

BASHIR SET the smartphone down on his bedside table, turned off the lamp, and lay back down. What time was it in Iraq? Morning. The sun would already be up. He pictured his wife in the kitchen, preparing breakfast for their two daughters. This plan needed to work. He'd been stuck in this backwater long enough. He needed to be home, fighting the real fight, making his name so that he could get a place on the Caliphate Council. It was a position he deserved. They could give Gomez a little more time, but they couldn't risk the Americans getting control of the mine before they did, or the Americans would be the only people to have access to the hafnium. They and their friends.

This business was already too time sensitive. The window for mining the ore would close as soon as the Chileans and Bolivians reached an agreement on their mutual border. Bribery could only hold off an agreement for so long. The Caliphate wouldn't be able to stand up to the Chilean or Bolivian army, not this far from their main forces. And they couldn't afford to disrupt the drug trade. It was a major source of the money they needed to wage jihad.

The Chileans or Bolivians would definitely choose the Americans as a mining partner over the Caliphate. So the sooner we start mining, the more hafnium we'll be able to extract before the Americans take over. And every pound of the ore that we ship will give us leverage to make new partners and to help our friends. That would be a great advantage in the jihad ahead. He would call Saad in the morning. They needed to start making preparations to take the mine if the villagers keep dragging their feet.

MEANWHILE, Gomez made his way down the meandering trail to the street through the center of the village. If only the men voted—it was only in extraordinary circumstance that women were allowed to vote —there would be thirty-one voters. Probably around twenty would vote for mining, so that was certain. But how many would choose the Americans? Perhaps ten or twelve would never vote for the gringos. Particularly those who blamed them for overturning the elected socialist Chilean government. And he could count on his cousin and one uncle and a nephew. So it was possible to turn the village to the Caliphate. It was a shame Rodriguez was still alive. She'd wormed her way into the village, but that was her, not her consortium. If she was dead, the Americans wouldn't stand a chance of winning the mining contract.

He got to his one-room clay brick house, went inside, and lit a kerosene lamp. Double his fee. He could start over. Go back to Iquique, quit transporting drugs, open a shop or a restaurant. Win his wife back or find a new woman—a woman who'd appreciate his abilities and be loyal to him. He set the lamp on the table in the center of the room. Maybe he didn't have to persuade the village men to choose the Caliphate to do the mining. Maybe Saad would pay him double his fee for the location of the mine. But that might be a step too far. The village elders, even his cousins, would see that as a betrayal. Still, the Americans already knew. He'd just be leveling the playing field. But he couldn't go through Saad for this. He'd need to deal with Commander Bashir. And if Bashir promised not to take the mine by force, what real harm would it cause? The Muslims always kept their word. Besides, if he had the money, he could leave Agua Dulce for good. There was nothing here for him except bad memories and poverty. He sat down in a straight-backed chair and took off his shoes. Maybe it would work. Maybe he'd finally get what he was due.

But first, before he started his negotiations with the commander, he needed to eliminate Rodriguez. Getting rid of her would prove to Bashir that he was a serious man, that kind of man he could make a deal with.

4

The next morning, Rodriguez put her Glock in her shoulder bag and went into the village to visit with Tomas and Roberto. Villagers were outside in front of every house, doing household chores or watching small children. It was a shame that she had to start carrying a gun, but something was changing in the village, something that had caused someone to attack her. Were the villagers closer to making a decision than she thought? Or was someone's paranoia about possibly losing the mining contract finally getting the best of them?

First she stopped at Tomas and Maria's house. They were both in their yard, Tomas sitting in a straight-backed chair writing in a ledger while his wife worked at her loom, a granddaughter sitting beside her.

Rodriguez spoke to Tomas in Quechuan. "Good morning. I was hoping to talk with you. Is this a good time?"

"Of course, of course." He gestured toward an empty chair.

Maria glanced over. "Good morning."

"Good morning."

Marie pointed to her head. "Did you have an accident?"

"Yes."

"Would you like me to look at it?"

"Don't bother yourself. It looks worse than it is."

Tomas continued. "How can I help you?"

"There was a village meeting last night."

"Nothing has been decided."

"I know it's hard for you to make a decision about the mining. I just wondered if there was anything I could explain to help you make up your mind."

"My hesitancy doesn't have anything to do with the practicalities. You've answered all our questions."

"Then what?"

He sighed. "I'm sure you've heard this story. At the beginning of time, the spirits put the crystals in the mountain. One day an earthquake opened the mountain and exposed the crystals. As soon as our people saw them, they knew they were a sacred gift and built the temple over them to honor the spirits and keep the crystals hidden." He reached into his pocket and took out a small silver disk with a purple zircon crystal set in the center. "We make these talismans to protect our families and our village. That's why our village has prospered, and our water has remained sweet, when so many other villages have died. We have always kept the mine secret, even from the beginning of the Spanish times. Only now has our secret gotten out. Will the telling of this secret be the end of our village? Only the spirits know."

"We mean you no harm."

"That doesn't mean you will not cause harm."

"You can't go back in time. All you can do is find the best way forward."

He nodded. "For us, all of us together must decide. That takes time."

"I understand. You want consensus."

"More than consensus. We believe that decision we make together will be the best decision." He waved her away. "Go in peace."

"Go in peace."

She continued down the street toward the plaza in front of the abandoned church. As she walked through the village, nodding and smiling to the men and women who were out in their yards, she saw Juan Carlos, the trader, drive into the village in a utility van fitted out as a rolling hardware store. He parked on the plaza. Villagers would come to the van later in the day to trade cloth and produce for shotgun shells, city hats and raincoats, and household items.

He'd been coming to the village for years, and before him, his father. He'd stay overnight in his van and leave tomorrow. Then he'd be back in a few weeks. The villagers said he was a fair trader. So there was nothing unusual about him being here. He was an outsider, but there was no way he was involved with the attack on her last night. He wanted the status quo, not the kind of progress that would lead to stores in the village that would ruin his trade, but his livelihood depended on the trust of the villagers. If that were broken, he wouldn't be welcome here.

She took the cross street to Roberto and Anna's house. Anna was sitting at her loom, her baby sleeping beside her and her toddler playing in the grass.

"Hey, Anna."

Anna replied in English. "Good morning, Cora."

"I brought something for little Roberto." She reached into her rucksack and took out a plastic figure of a squirrel. She held it up for Anna to see. Anna nodded. She stepped over to the toddler and crouched down. "For you," she said in Quechuan. The little boy smiled and grabbed the toy.

Rodriguez switched back to English. "Juan Carlos is in town. Are you going to buy anything?"

"Not this time. We're taking our trade goods to the market town next month. We'll make more."

"Always thinking of the future."

"We have to."

"Is your husband around?"

"In the garden."

Rodriguez walked around to the back of the clay brick house. Behind the pigsty, a four-foot-high fence of twisted branches marked out a large garden that ran back twenty feet. Roberto stood in the tall corn, green beans trellising up the stalks, hoeing the weeds. Rodriguez came in through the gate and walked down the row. "*Hola, Roberto.*"

"Good morning, Cora."

"Your garden looks good."

"Thank you. It's going to be a productive year."

"How did the meeting go last night?"

"Nothing is settled. But we're getting closer, I think."

"How so?"

"Even those who are most against change realize that the ore can't be kept a secret anymore. It's down to whether to mine."

"And who to trust."

"It's always about trust, Cora. Our people have been run over again and again, ever since the Spanish came."

"Any other potential partners?"

"Other than your American consortium? None I know about. But you know Tomas. He holds his cards close to his vest."

"Okay. Well, I'll let you get back to your work."

She started back down the street. Everything seemed to be going to plan, even if it was taking much longer than she expected. Eventually, Tomas would come around to accepting the inevitable, and Roberto and his allies would guide the villagers to accepting her proposal. Maybe sooner than later. In the meantime, she needed to be more careful. Her enemy might make another attempt. Tonight, before she went to bed, she would have to take precautions to guarantee her safety.

Roberto closed the gate to the garden and came around the house. Anna was still at her loom. He spoke in Quechuan. "Did Cora ask you anything?"

She shook her head. "No. How about you?"

"Just the usual questions about the process."

"What did you tell her?"

"Nothing specific. I did as we agreed. No one can know that we plan to leave here and go back to the US so we can find help for little Roberto, or they won't accept my advice."

"We have no choice. We can't afford the specialist doctors in Chile or Bolivia, but little Roberto is a US citizen. The doctors there have to help him. As soon as he's well, we can come home."

"I hope so."

"Cora says that Juan Carlos is in town."

"I'll go see him later."

MEANWHILE, Gomez stood in a clearing to the south of Rodriguez's cabin, talking with Alfredo. "Keep your voice down."

"I'm not trying again. She almost beat me last time, and I had all the advantage. If I go back, she'll be waiting for me with a pistol in her hand."

"Don't go inside," Gomez said. "I'll give you a gun. Shoot through the window. The walls are thick. They'll provide cover if she shoots back. When she tries to make a break for it, then you finish her."

"What if she doesn't come out?"

"Set the roof on fire."

"If it's so easy, why don't you do it?"

"Everyone will suspect me. I've spoken out against her from the beginning. I need an air-tight alibi."

"And you'll give me 89,000 Chilean pesos just for the attempt? No matter how it turns out?"

"You have my word."

Alfredo rubbed his chin. "Okay. I'll try, but I'm not guaranteeing anything."

"Do it soon."

"As soon as you give me the gun."

KD AND BLUNT, dressed as business travelers, were on an express train speeding south through France toward Spain. Their target,

Patrick Colbert, was in the train car in front of them. Tina had found out a lot about him since they'd started tracking him. Ex Foreign Legion, gun for hire, specialized in messy work. No wife, no children. Seemed to be mainly working for the Blaze Group right now. The world wouldn't miss him if they had to put him down.

"What do you think he knows?" Blunt asked.

"More than us," KD replied. "Blaze and Lysenko wouldn't be using the same safe house if they weren't connected somehow."

"Might not have anything to do with the hafnium."

"Might not. Colbert might have just been hired to kill us."

"Either way, after we take him, he's going to a black site."

"I hope we're not wasting our time. We need actionable intelligence on whoever is after the ore."

After the train pulled into the Lyon Part Dieu station, they watched Colbert hustle off and disappear into the crowd. They followed at a distance. "Have you got him?" KD said into the comms connected to her encrypted smartphone.

"Yes," Tina replied. "We're listening in via his phone. I'll keep you updated."

Colbert went to the taxi stand in front of the station and got into a taxi. Tina continued. "He's going to the Magpie Cafe."

KD and Blunt got in the next taxi, which navigated through the downtown traffic to an area of boutique shops along the Rhone River. As their taxi was pulling up in front of a white stone restaurant with a painting of a magpie over the glass double doors, Colbert went inside. KD and Blunt waited on the sidewalk for a minute before KD stepped inside to the hostess station and acted like she was reading a menu. Colbert was at a table in the back, where he was sitting with a large man with a bulbous nose and a gray beard.

KD went outside. Blunt was leaning against the wall a few doors down. "Looks like we're meeting a new player."

"We going to split up?"

She tapped her comms. "Tina, can you keep after Colbert?"

"As long as he's within range of a cell tower."

She turned back to Blunt. "Let's focus on the new guy."

. . .

COLBERT GLANCED around at the restaurant patrons sitting nearby and then smoothed the tablecloth with his hands. "So, Jacques, what's the job?"

"Never one to beat around the bush," Jacques replied. "Would you like something to drink?"

"No, thank you."

"On to business then. We're moving a large order of Soviet era AK-47s. Almost untraceable, which is why we want to make sure they're not hijacked. They're in a warehouse in Madrid. We're trucking them to our warehouse at the port in Barcelona, where they'll be loaded on a cargo ship. We want you riding with the driver."

"Do you know there's going to be an attempt?"

"No. We're just taking precautions."

"Okay, then."

Jacques passed him a note. "Here's the address in Madrid."

"Tell Blaze I'm expecting my money."

"I've got nothing to do with that, but I'll pass your message along."

"You do that."

KD AND BLUNT watched Colbert leave the restaurant and get into a taxi. KD spoke into her comms. "What have you got for us, Tina?"

"New player's first name is Jacques. He sent Colbert to a warehouse in Madrid. I'll email the details as we get them."

"What can you tell us about Jacques?"

"I need a clear photo to run him through the database."

KD and Blunt crossed the street to a small park along the river. When Jacques came out of the restaurant, Blunt took several pictures of him with his smartphone and emailed them to Tina. "One of those work?"

"There're two good ones here. I'll be in touch as soon as I know something. It can take a little longer when I only have the first name."

KD and Blunt followed Jacques down the street to a small hotel with a 1930s façade, wrought iron balcony over a wide marble entryway, located across from another small park. Blunt sat down on a bench with a good view of the front of the hotel. KD went around the corner to a café and came back with to-go coffee. An hour later, Tina called KD on her encrypted line.

"Your new guy goes by the name Jacques Athos."

"Athos? You mean like the three musketeers?"

"Exactly."

"No real name?"

"That's it. He's a known Lysenko associate."

"So we're moving up the food chain. Lysenko and Blaze seem to be intertwined on something. Have we got anyone in Lyon who can help us?"

"Closest I've got is someone in Paris, if Assistant Director Garcia agrees."

"Too far away. We'll have to improvise. Keep a close watch on Colbert." KD ended the call and filled in Blunt.

Blunt gestured toward the hotel. "How long do you want to stay here?"

"Colbert will be in Madrid tomorrow. He'll be traveling with the arms shipment the day after that. If we could catch him with the shipment, we could roll him up. And he might flip."

"Maybe."

"But if Athos is on the move tomorrow, we might find out more about Lysenko's network. And maybe that would get us closer to finding out if jihadis are in the mix or if they're just a red herring."

"So we stay here until tomorrow," Blunt said. "You want first watch or second?"

"You go to dinner and come back, then I'll leave, find a hotel, and come back for second watch."

"Get one with a decent bed."

"Only the best for you, partner."

5

B ack at Agua Dulce, well after dark, Juan Carlos closed the
sides on his van. He'd had a successful day. The cloth and
the blankets were always particularly fine in this village.
He'd caught up on all the gossip, including the movements of the
American, but he still hadn't heard from his contact. As he started to
sit down in a folding chair in the light of a camp lantern, a man
stepped out of the shadows. "Roberto."

They shook hands.

The trader spoke in Spanish. "I was afraid you weren't coming."

"The neighbors on my street were out late."

They stepped into the shadows around the side of the van.

"What do you have for me?" Juan Carlos asked.

"The people met last night. Eventually they will decide to mine
the ore, but they're not there yet."

"What about the geologist?"

"She's waiting for the people to reach a decision."

"Will the Americans get the contract?"

"They're the obvious partners right now, but if others make a bid,
the one who will provide the most benefit to the village will get the
contract."

"Even though the Americans know where the mine is?"

"I don't know how many Americans know where the mine is. Senora Rodriguez knows, but she promised not to tell. Besides, once the mining starts, it won't be a secret anymore."

"But you won't tell anyone beforehand."

"No.

"So the contract is still open."

"Until the people decide."

"Thank you, my friend. I've got something for you."

"What?"

"Satellite phone." Juan Carlos opened the passenger's door on his van and brought out a small black case and handed it to Roberto. "As soon as you know that your people have decided to mine, you call the number on this phone and tell the person who answers. Then you'll get your first payment. If my friends get to make a bid, you'll get another. And who knows? If my friends get the contract, you might be getting payments for the foreseeable future."

"As soon as I know anything, I'll call."

Juan Carlos watched Roberto slip away into the shadows before he climbed into the van, got out his own satellite phone, and made a call.

"It's about time I heard from you," Lysenko said.

"I couldn't come here earlier than usual. That would be suspicious."

"So what do you know?"

"The American geologist spends her time at the ruins."

"But the mine?"

"It's here somewhere. The villagers had a meeting. They still haven't decided whether or not to mine."

"But you don't know where the mine is?"

"The villagers are closemouthed about it. No one will tell where it is."

"Not even Roberto?"

"He's not going to tell until the partner is selected and he's gotten his payoff. And I can't try to incentivize any of the others without tipping my hand."

"But the mine is near the village?"

"Must be."

"And you can't find it?"

"I haven't seen anyone going anywhere unusual."

"But the villagers are going to decide to mine the ore?"

"Yes, that's what Roberto thinks. I've given him a satellite phone. As soon as he knows anything, he'll call you. Do you want me to come back in two weeks?"

"No, I'll deal with Roberto from now on. Your payment will be wired to your account." Lysenko ended the call.

Juan Carlos put away his satellite phone. Easy money. But why was a black marketeer interested in an old mine in the mountains? And why was everyone keeping its location a secret? Juan Carlos got out of his van, sat down in the folding chair, and stretched out his legs. Lysenko was a dangerous man. Better just to take his money and not to ask questions.

LYSENKO LAY his satellite phone down on his desk. He was sitting in his office in Warsaw, Poland, his lieutenant for Eastern Europe, Jan Kowalski, sitting on the other side of his glass-topped desk. "The ore is there, and the American is still there."

"And they know where the mine is."

Lysenko nodded. "Yes, somehow they won the trust of the villagers. But the villagers still haven't decided what they'll do. The longer they stall, the more parties are going to find out about the hafnium and take an interest."

"Why are we switching sides?"

"From the New Islamic Caliphate to the Blaze Group? Our position hasn't changed. We want access to the hafnium. There's a lot of money to be made, and we'll make more with the Blaze Group. We're getting the Caliphate the arms shipment they wanted. Those Soviet weapons will give them deniability across most of the

Middle East. And they're used to sacrificing their own for the greater good. They'll forgive us for betraying them when we give them access to the refined hafnium and they don't have to process it themselves."

"But we're waiting until the Caliphate has the mine?"

"If we find out the exact location of the mine first, then no. But if they find out first, we'll let them show us where it is and take it from them."

"What about the Chilean and Bolivian governments?"

"I don't care how much negotiating the Americans do, neither is going to agree to give the mine to the other. There's too much unknown and too much at stake. Besides, Blaze claims to own two of the negotiators, which should slow things down even more. It could be years before they come to a resource-sharing agreement."

"But they could reach an agreement on protecting the mine from outsiders at any time. That would benefit both of them."

"That's why our best strategy is to start mining as soon as possible. Where's our nearest concentration of mercenaries?"

"We've got a crew in Ciudad del Este, Paraguay, protecting our arms business in the tri border area."

Lysenko pulled up a map of the area on his computer. "Too far to drive across Paraguay and Bolivia."

Kowalski pointed to a spot on the map near the border of Chile and Bolivia. "We could use the old smugglers' airstrip on the Bolivian side, drop in the equipment and land the men."

"What condition is it in?"

"I don't know."

"Have someone check it out. And be ready to move as soon as we know the location of the mine or the Caliphate's people take it."

"I'll start assembling the men and materials." Kowalski stood up to leave.

"And have my jet put on standby."

"You're going to South America?"

"I'm not letting anyone screw this up. I'm going to oversee this personally."

. . .

ROBERTO TURNED RIGHT at the plaza and made his way down the starlit cross street until he reached his house. Anna was sitting at the table, her book pushed up close to the kerosene lamp. She had already put the children to bed.

She looked up. "There you are. How did it go?"

"Very well. Juan Carlos gave me a satellite phone. We get our first payment when the people decide to mine and another if Juan Carlos's friends get to make a bid."

"Will it be enough?"

"If we're careful, we should be able to make the trip. Get a tourist visa and fly in like we did last time. Once we're there, I'll try to get my old job back working construction."

"The boss liked you."

"If they need workers, I ought to be able to get a job."

"Maybe our luck is changing."

"Maybe it is. Maybe the US doctors will really be able to figure out what's wrong with little Roberto."

GOMEZ AND ALFREDO stood in the dark on the footpath that led from the village up to Rodriguez's cabin.

"Do you have it?"

Gomez took a Glock pistol out of a bag and handed it to his cousin. "Just like what the gangsters and the gringos use. No one will know it was you."

Alfredo started up the path to Rodriguez's cabin. Gomez took off in the opposite direction. When he reached the main street in the village, he saw that Juan Carlos was still sitting outside his van on the plaza in front of the church. The perfect alibi. Gomez hurried down the street to the van.

"Juan Carlos, I'm glad you're still up."

"What can I do for you?"

"You don't happen to have a newspaper?"

"Last week's." He dug around to the front of his van. "You can have it."

"Thanks so much."

MEANWHILE, Alfredo slipped up on Rodriguez's cabin. No light seeped out from the edges of the door or the closed window shutters. He moved slowly and carefully, expecting boobytraps, but he found none. When he reached the cabin, he did what Gomez had suggested, moving around the side of the cabin and firing through the shutters three times in rapid succession.

RODRIGUEZ LAY in her sleeping bag on the ground on the other side of a group of dense shrubs behind her cabin. She peered into the dark, gripping her pistol and listening for movement after the gunfire stopped. Someone was at her cabin. Someone who was not taking chances this time. Now would be the time to catch them off guard. She wriggled out of her sleeping bag and crept silently around the shrubs.

ALFREDO WENT AROUND to the front of the cabin and listened at the door. Nothing. He tried the doorknob, and slowly pushed the door open. He couldn't see anything in the black. He lit a match. The room was empty. He shut the door and started down the hill, the pistol at his side.

WHEN ALFREDO FIRED THE GLOCK, Gomez looked off up the hill. "What's that?

"I don't know," Juan Carlos replied. "Sounded like a gun."

"A gun? Hard to believe. Whatever it was, it stopped. Thanks for the newspaper." He walked off down the street toward his house.

About halfway home, he saw his cousin come down off the footpath that went up the hill. He hurried to catch up. "Well, is it done?"

"There was no one there," Alfredo said.

"No one there?"

"I shot through the window shutters. There was no response, so I opened the door. No one was there."

"Give me the gun."

Alfredo handed him the gun. "Will you keep your word?"

"About the money? Yes. A promise is a promise. You want cash?"

"Yes."

"When I go to market day, I'll get the money from the bank."

"Don't forget."

"I won't."

RODRIGUEZ CROUCHED in the tall weeds beside the path, watching the man who'd shot up her cabin. He was talking to someone. When he turned, she saw his face. It couldn't be, but it was. Gomez. Tomas's cousin. He was outspoken against her and the American consortium. He wanted her to leave. The first attempt could have been just to try to scare her, but now it was clear he wanted to murder her. Why? Who was he working for? Should she tell Tomas? Or Roberto, for that matter? Why should they believe her? It would sound like she was making something up to try to discredit Gomez. She needed more proof. She stayed in her spot until Gomez and his friend went their separate ways. Then she went back up the path to her cabin, staying in the deep shadow. Tomorrow, she needed to think about improving her security, but tonight she was going back to her sleeping bag in the bushes.

WHEN GOMEZ GOT BACK to his one-room clay brick house, he sat at the table near the cook stove and started reading the week-old newspaper he'd gotten from Juan Carlos, but he couldn't concentrate. Rodriguez was still alive. She'd definitely be on her guard now. He wouldn't get another chance to kill her. But the fee that Saad had promised him for winning the contract kept jumping to the front of his mind. The village men were so slow to make up their minds, and when they finally decided, they could decide the wrong way and give the contract to the Americans. It could happen. It was a possibility.

He rolled up the newspaper and rapped it against the table. But if he could make a deal with Commander Bashir, the money for the location of the mine, all his problems would go away. In all his dealings with the Muslims, they'd never broken their word. Maybe Bashir wouldn't want to make a deal, but the only way to find out was to ask.

He got out his satellite phone and called Saad.

"Do you have news?"

"Nothing has changed since yesterday."

"Then why are you calling?"

"You said that you would double my fee if I got you the mining contract."

"Yes."

"Would you pay that money for the location of the mine?"

"You know where it is?"

"All the villagers know."

"Then why haven't you already told me?"

"Because everyone agreed to keep the secret, and I didn't want to betray their trust."

"But you will now?"

"As soon as the villagers make their decision, everyone will know anyway. But if you want to know now, so you'll be ready to move, I'll tell you."

"Yes, if the mine is where you say it is, I'll double your fee."

"I have to hear Commander Bashir say it."

"I speak for the commander."

"This is too important to trust with anyone except him."

"Okay, he'll call you in a few minutes."

SAAD CALLED Bashir on his smartphone and filled him in.

"He's known all along?"

"Evidently."

"And he wouldn't tell because he didn't want to betray the village's trust?"

"That's what he said. But everything has a price."

"In this case, twice his promised fee. This is a bold move on his part. We need to start keeping an eye on him. What's his sat phone number?"

BASHIR CALLED GOMEZ. "We will pay you double your fee for the location of the mine."

"I have one condition," Gomez said.

"Name it."

"You must swear by all you hold dear that you will not take the mine by force or tell anyone else where it is."

"I swear by Allah and the lives of my children."

Gomez took a deep breath. "The mine is inside the temple ruins."

"The ruins at the top of the hill?"

"Yes."

"Really?"

"A shaft at the back of the antechamber leads to the mine face."

"As soon as I see the mine with my own eyes, you'll be paid."

"Remember, you gave your word. You cannot take the mine by force."

"I promise."

GOMEZ ENDED THE CALL. He's done it. There was no turning back. He was going to have enough money to start over. And all he'd done was share information that the Americans already had. He didn't see how the location of the mine could help Bashir since he'd promised not to take it by force, but that wasn't his problem. Now all he had to do was be patient until Commander Bashir saw the mine for himself and paid him.

.   .   .

THE NEXT MORNING, Rodriguez crawled out of her sleeping bag in the bushes, shook the bag out, and carried it back to her cabin. The closed shutters on the south window were marked by three bullet holes. Inside, after she turned on her camping lantern, she found a bullet hole in the blanket on her bed and another one in the table. The third bullet had gone into the plank floor.

She rolled up her sleeping bag and laid it on a chair. She needed to start documenting what was happening if she was going to eventually convince the villagers. She walked down the path into the village. At the Sinchis' house, Maria was at her loom in the front yard. Rodriguez spoke in Quechuan. "Good morning, Maria. Is your husband at home?"

She called back into the house. Tomas came out on the stoop. "Cora, how can I help you?"

"I've got something to show you."

"Very well, let me get my hat."

He went into the house and came out wearing a wide-brimmed hat. "What's this all about?"

"It would just be better to show you."

"All right."

They walked up the path to Rodriguez's cabin. "Last night, someone shot into my cabin."

"What?"

"Look here." She showed him the bullet holes in the shutters.

He examined the raw wood at the edges of the holes. "These are new."

"Please come inside."

They went into the cabin. She opened the shutters to let in more light. Then she pointed to her cot. "Here."

"May I?"

She nodded.

He pulled back the blanket, saw the hole in the mattress, and got down on his hands and knees to look at the ground under the cot.

"Went right through."

She nodded.

He stood up and looked at the table. "A second one here."

She pointed to the bullet hole in the floor. "And the third one there."

He looked from the window to the bed. "Where were you?"

"I was hiding in the bushes."

"So you were expecting trouble?"

"Yes."

"Some might say you did this yourself to stir up trouble."

"I know."

"Who do you think did this?"

"I don't have any idea."

"Do you want me to bring it to the village council?"

"Not yet. Maybe someone was just trying to scare me."

"This looks like more than that."

"I agree. I just think I need more proof before I take it to the council."

"What are you going to do now?"

"Go about my business."

"I'll talk with Maria. You can stay at our house."

"No, I'm going to stay here. If someone is trying to hurt me, I don't want to put you at risk."

"Are you sure? It's no trouble."

"I'm sure."

"Let me know if you change your mind." Tomas started back down the hill.

Rodriguez watched him walk down the path. She had one surveillance camera in her gear. She could set it up to record the area in front of the door, but even that wouldn't provide conclusive evidence unless the person recorded was holding a gun out as if they were going to fire it. And even if she wore her Kevlar vest and slept under the bed, there was no guarantee that the last thing she wouldn't hear would be a gunshot.

She closed the cabin door. Who was the guy Gomez sent to kill

"Gunshots? I heard some loud popping while I was talking with Juan Carlos. He also thought they were gunshots, but I don't know. Seems unlikely."

"Yes."

"So you were at the temple?"

Tomas nodded.

"Did the spirits tell you how to vote?"

"No, not yet."

"Well, maybe they're not going to tell you."

"Maybe. Or maybe they will speak to me tomorrow. Only time will tell. Later."

Tomas continued down the street. So Gomez couldn't have fired the shots because he was with Juan Carlos when the shots were fired. Unless they were both in on it, which was ludicrous. Of course, Gomez had always been sneaky, even as a boy. Maybe he got someone else to do the shooting while he set his alibi. Shooting someone from hiding was not as difficult as standing in front of them. But, really, it was all too crazy. If he hadn't seen the bullet holes, he'd never have believed it had happened.

6

Early the next morning in Lyon, KD and Blunt sat in a rental car across the street from Athos's hotel, drinking coffee and eating croissants out of paper bags. Shortly after 10:00 a.m., a red Audi pulled up in front of the hotel and Athos came out the hotel pulling a roller bag and got into the back seat. KD and Blunt started after the Audi, Blunt driving.

The Audi moved quickly, slightly above the speed limit, weaving through the city traffic. "They either know we're on them or they were expecting a tail," KD said.

"They're not going to spot me," Blunt replied.

At a packed intersection, the Audi raced through a yellow light. Blunt stepped on the gas, and shot through the intersection as the light turned red.

"Close call," KD said.

"I had a few more seconds."

The Audi slid around the next right turn, entered an alley, swerved around a car parked up on the curb, and turned left at the end of the block. Blunt was three cars behind. The Audi sped through the next intersection, and a utility van slid crosswise to the street, blocking both lanes. Blunt braked hard. A guy in coveralls in the van's passenger seat showed a machine pistol. KD and Blunt ducked in their seats. Cars honked behind them. When they sat up, the van was gone.

"That's that," Blunt said.

"Wonder when they made us?"

"I bet he spotted us when he came out of the hotel."

"You think so? Let's return this rental. See if we can capture Colbert and seize Lysenko's arms shipment."

Blunt turned right at the next intersection.

"Need me to set up a route on my phone?"

"No, I've got it. The rental place wasn't that far from the hotel."

KD called Tina and filled her in. "I'm still tracking Colbert via his phone," Tina said. "As long as he doesn't change phones, I know where he is."

"Is he transporting the shipment yet?"

"No, he's still at a hotel in Madrid."

"Okay. Is Garcia available?"

"Hold on." The line was quiet for a few minutes. "I'm connecting you."

"Hello?"

"Garcia? KD here."

"How long were you planning to galivant around Europe?"

"We're making progress, boss."

"So why are we talking?"

"We're going to need back up to take down a gun smuggling operation in Spain." KD filled in the details about their activities.

"Okay," Garcia said. "I'll get in touch with my contact at the Guardia Civil."

ATHOS CALLED Lysenko from the back of the Audi. "Somebody was tailing me this morning. Black man and a white woman. They handled themselves pretty well, but we got rid of them."

"Do you think they know about the shipment?"

"I don't know. I gave the information to Colbert. Do you want me to call it off?"

"If the shipment isn't delivered to the cargo ship, it'll be another month before we can get rid of it. The Caliphate doesn't want to wait that long. Call Colbert on the burner. Tell him to expect trouble. He can do whatever he thinks best as long as the shipment gets delivered to the port in time."

THE SUN WAS up when Rodriguez crawled out of her sleeping bag in the bushes behind her cabin, turned on her tablet computer, and downloaded the surveillance footage from the camera she'd hidden above her door. Nothing. She picked up her sleeping bag and walked around to the front of the cabin. The small piece of tape she'd stuck across the bottom of the door jamb was still in place. No one had slipped by the camera. She went inside.

Was Gomez still after her? Or was he done trying to kill her? And if he was done, was it because he thought he'd lost his chance, or because he'd found a way to move on with his plan without killing her? No way to tell. Not without more information.

After she changed clothes and ate breakfast, she walked down into Agua Dulce, smiling and waving at the villagers working outside in their yards, stopping occasionally to chat, keeping to her habit of going to the temple to document the interior, all the while trying to think of how she could keep track of Gomez's movements. The village was small. Everyone knew everyone else's business. Someone was bound to notice if she changed her routine. Still, it was worth the risk.

After she got up to the temple, she looked around to make sure no one was there talking to the spirits, and then she snuck down the hill, staying off the path, making her way silently through the brush and trees. When she reached the bottom of the hill, she continued around the back side of the church and along the ravine until she was behind Gomez's house. She peeked around the side. Gomez was sitting in the front yard, talking with one of Tomas's grandsons. Was he the one who'd shot at her? Too tall and too thin.

She heard talking to her right. Gomez's neighbors. She'd be seen if she stayed here. And if Gomez left his house, there was no way she could follow without attracting attention. But the lack of privacy worked both ways. Gomez could plot against her during the day, but he could only act against her after dark. That was the only way he could be sure of not being seen. She snuck back the way she'd come, went into the temple, turned on the spotlights, and continued documenting the wall paintings.

That evening after dark she snuck down from her cabin to Gomez's house. Light shined around the edges of the windows and doors. She slipped up to the back window and listened. She could hear movement inside. Was Gomez going to stay in all evening? Would he have visitors? She sat down under the window and waited.

THE NEXT DAY, KD and Blunt sat in an unmarked police car with their Guardia Civil contact Captain Ramon Franco on the right of way on the A2 freeway an hour out from Barcelona. A team of three unmarked police cars had been tracking the tractor-trailer of Soviet AK-47s ever since it left the Madrid warehouse. The tractor-trailer rolled by their position, and they fell in behind it.

"Everything is prepared," Captain Franco said. "An assault team is on standby. As soon as we know the location of the warehouse, they'll move in."

"You get the warehouse, the weapons, maybe even the freighter," KD said. "We get Colbert."

"But we get him back when you're done."

"Absolutely."

"We've been waiting for an opportunity like this for a long time. If this smuggling ring is as powerful as you say, this investigation could ferret out significant corruption at the port."

"It'll be front page news."

As they followed the tractor-trailer through the city to a row of warehouses along the shipping port, the police van containing the assault team fell in behind them. They were all half a block back when the tractor-trailer turned into a two-story, rusted sheet metal building. The overhead doors rolled down behind it.

The three unmarked police cars parked behind the warehouse. Six Guardia Civil officers got out of the unmarked cars, took their Kevlar vests from the trunks, and strapped them on before they set a perimeter. Captain Franco's unmarked police car and the assault team van blocked the street in front of the warehouse. KD, Blunt, and Captain Franco got out of their car but crouched behind their open car doors. The assault team, Kevlar armor and assault rifles, formed up behind shields.

Captain Franco spoke over the car's loudspeaker. "Warehouse. You are surrounded. Come out with your hands up."

There was no response.

Captain Franco spoke again.

Two men tried to escape by climbing out a side window, but they were captured as they tried to run through the back lot. The assault team moved forward in formation, shields in front.

A burst of automatic gunfire from a second-floor window ricocheted across the pavement in front of the assault team. Two of the team laid down cover fire while the rest of the team rushed the pedestrian door next to the overhead door, kicked it in, and threw flashbang grenades into the warehouse. Then they entered the building. The men on the first floor dropped their guns and raised their hands.

KD and Blunt came into the building behind the assault team, found the stairs, and made their way up to the second floor. They moved along the hallway opening doors, but every room was empty. On their way down, they saw Captain Franco at the bottom of the stairs. "All clear," KD said.

"We've got them all," Captain Franco said.

Three tractor-trailers sat in a row. Seven men sat on the concrete in front of the trucks surrounded by Guardia Civil officers holding their assault rifles at the ready. Blunt looked through the prisoners. "He's not here."

"Check the trailers," KD said.

KD, Blunt, and two Guardia Civil officers opened the backs of the trailers. The one they'd been following contained crates of Soviet-made AK-47s. The next one contained body armor and uniforms, and the last one contained flatscreen TVs, but no Colbert. "No one escaped," Captain Franco said. "So he's got to be here. Let's start at the front and work our way back." He pointed to two of his officers. "You two with me."

Captain Franco started on the left, while KD and Blunt started on the right. They worked their ways down the sides of the warehouse, looking in every locker or crate large enough to hold a person.

MEANWHILE, Colbert was clinging to the underside of the leftmost tractor-trailer. He'd seen the two American agents he's tried to kill in Washington, DC. How had they traced him here? He couldn't let them capture him. Time was running out. Once Captain Franco's group had gone by his position, he dropped to the floor and scrambled out from under the trailer, his pistol in his hand. As the Guardia Civil officers spun toward him, he opened fire, then shot through a side window and dived out into the alley, rolled across the pavement, and clambered to his feet.

Two officers were chasing and firing at him as he ran out of the alley, crossed the wharf, and dove into the ocean. He swam furiously, bullets cutting through the water all around him. He dove deep, using a dolphin kick to go under a small boat, came up for air, and dove again.

KD AND BLUNT watched Colbert disappear underwater the second time. "No blood in the water," Blunt said.

"You can't beat luck," KD said. She called over to Captain Franco. "He's gone."

Captain Franco ordered his men to cease fire. Then he got out his phone and ordered a door-to-door search of the surrounding neighborhood. "Maybe we'll find him."

They went back into the warehouse. "I know your man got away, but we've got three tractor-trailers of contraband and nine prisoners. No fatalities. Even if we don't capture him, this is a good day's work, my friends."

"We needed that man," KD said. "But it is what it is. Thanks for your help."

"My pleasure."

"Can we get a ride to the airport?"

"I'll have one of the unmarked cars take you."

"Get in touch if you find him."

"Of course."

Captain Franco called over one of his men.

As KD, Blunt, and the officer were walking out the back of the warehouse, KD called Tina to fill her in.

"His phone is dead," she replied.

"Any way to track him?"

"We'll automate a facial recognition program on the public surveillance cameras around his likely locations, but that's so much computing that we won't be able to do it for more than a few days. So if he goes to ground, we'll have to wait for him to go through passport control at a major point of entry where we have some sway."

"He won't go through Paris again."

"It's all we can do. Maybe we'll get lucky."

At the airport, KD and Blunt sat in the back corner of a tapas restaurant, eating dinner while they waited for their flight back to Washington, DC, when KD got a phone call from Tina.

"That guy Blunt recognized on the surveillance footage that got us on to Lysenko?"

"Yeah?" KD asked.

"His name's Creston. CIA tipped the Irish police, who picked him up in Ireland."

"Are we going to get a chance to talk to him?"

"Garcia's working on it now, so sit tight."

"Thanks."

KD filled in Blunt.

"Hope he gets an open cage in Guantanamo," Blunt said. "Hope they throw away the key."

"That bad?"

"That bad."

"So what happened on the op that went so wrong?"

"Truth be told, we had bad intel, went in undermanned. Lysenko hired some Mafia goons. We got caught in a crossfire at the pickup location. Two of our guys went down fast. Creston executed them while they were on the ground. Our undercover—a guy who'd been in Lysenko's crew for over a year—was found in a ditch three days later. Had to use his dental records to identify him. You know, Doc, some crooks are crooks, and some are rotten bastards. That's the kind we're dealing with here."

"Well, if Lysenko and Blaze were really involved in trying to steal the hafnium sample, if we haven't just been chasing our tails, maybe we'll get a chance to nail him this time."

KD got another call from Tina. "Yeah?"

"Check your email. I've got you on the next flight to Dublin. Creston pissed off the Irish big time. You're getting thirty minutes in a hotel room at the airport."

AFTER DARK, Colbert climbed up the side of a speed boat, rolled over onto the deck, and lay there, catching his breath. He been in the water a long time, but he was certain that he'd outrun the police. He glanced at the nearby boats. He couldn't see anyone. Still, he crawled to the door to the cabin, broke the lock on the door, and stepped down into the cabin, where he found dry clothes in a locker.

After he changed clothes, he emptied the pockets of his wet pants. Phone was a total loss. He went through his wallet. His driver's license and credit cards were fine, but his paper cards and cash were soaked.

He made a quick search of the cabin and found a bag to put his wet clothes, phone, and wallet into. He came out on the deck and glanced around before he set off down the dock toward the wharf.

There was a convenience store at the end of the wharf by the parking lot. Bored clerk standing behind the checkout counter. Two teenagers buying chips. He used the payphone in the corner to call a number he'd memorized.

"Hello?"

"I'm compromised."

"Is this a public number?"

"Yes."

"I'll call you right back."

Colbert hung up the phone. A few minutes later it rang. He picked it up. "Yeah?"

"Where are you?"

"I'm at a private marina north of the shipping port in Barcelona."

"What's your situation?"

"I'm on the move. The shipment was lost."

"We heard."

"The two American agents from the botched job in Washington, DC, were at the warehouse."

"At the warehouse?"

"Yeah, I'll be back in touch when I'm in the clear."

"Good luck."

LYSENKO AND JACQUES ATHOS sat in Lysenko's office in Warsaw. "How did the Spanish get onto the AK-47s?"

"I don't know, boss. Maybe it had something to do with the American agents who were tailing me."

"How did they get onto you?"

"I met with three operatives in the last week. I didn't see anyone suspicious until after I met with Colbert."

"The American agents must have followed him from Washington."

"Maybe."

"Colbert was at the Munich safehouse. Shut it down just to be sure."

"That will be a pain in the ass."

"I don't care. If it's bugged, it's worse than useless."

"I'll make the call. What do you want to do about Colbert? He's on the run."

"We knew he might have trouble. We gambled and lost. If he doesn't get captured, he could still be useful."

"But if the Spanish get him?"

"Then we'll have to eliminate him."

"I'll start looking around for an independent contractor in case we need one."

"Okay, that's the past. What about the future? Where can we get another shipment of Soviet weapons?"

"That's hard, boss. Almost too difficult anymore."

"Well, the shipment the Spanish took is going into the smelter. What about that Israeli trader? Doesn't he have access to a supply?"

"They've been cracking down on corruption. It might be possible to get Soviet AK-47s next year, but not anytime soon."

"Nothing left in Kazakhstan?"

"Nothing we can get our hands on. The current government hates us."

"There must be a supply somewhere. I don't want to tell the Caliphate we can't fill their order. And I don't want to give them their money back."

"I'll make some calls." He stood up. "What do you want to do about the Americans?"

"If you get a chance, kill them."

7

W hen KD and Blunt landed in Dublin, two plainclothes detectives, dark suits and raincoats, met them at the gate. "Thorne and Blunt?" the nearest man asked.

KD nodded her head.

"I'm Inspector Jennings and this is Sergeant Michaels. We're with the Special Detective Unit."

Everyone showed their IDs.

"Follow me," Jennings continued. They started down the concourse.

Jennings ran a magnetic strip card through the card reader on a security door. "We've got a car on the tarmac. We'll take you into the hotel through the service entrance."

They went down the stairs to a black Ford Focus, Michaels driving, Jennings in the front passenger's seat. Michaels followed the marked lanes painted on the asphalt out to a security gate and down the airport road past long-term parking to the rear of a hotel.

"What condition is Creston in?" Blunt asked. "We haven't been briefed on his arrest."

"He's scuffed up a bit," Jennings replied. "Resisting arrest and so forth, but he's well able to answer your questions, if he wants to."

"What charges is he facing here?"

"Weapons smuggling."

They parked next to the dumpster behind the hotel and went in the service entrance to the service elevator.

"You'll have him on your own. We have a surveillance camera set up in the room, so we'll be able to see and hear everything. If you get too rough, we'll put a stop to it."

"Fair enough," KD replied.

They went down the hall to a hotel room where a burly uniformed officer stood in front of the door. "Sir," the officer said. He opened the door.

Inside, another officer sat in the desk chair, and Creston, hands cuffed behind his back, sat on the bed watching a soccer match on the TV.

"Creston," Blunt said, "good to see you."

"Oh, shit, US feds," Creston said. He turned to the officer sitting in the desk chair. "You're not going to leave me with them, are you?"

The officer got up from the chair and turned off the TV. The Irish police left the room. Creston looked from Blunt to KD.

"We've come a long way," KD said. "No one knows we're here. We know you were at the safehouse in Augsburg. We know Colbert was there."

"So? I'm not going to say anything that might incriminate me."

"We don't care about you. You're going to be an old man when you get out of prison here."

"Then why should I say anything?"

"Because we could extradite you after you've served your sentence here. Turn you over to the CIA for enhanced interrogation.

"You're bluffing."

She shook her head. "Why was Colbert there?"

Creston sighed. "He came to pick up a phone."

"But he works for Blaze, doesn't he?"

"The boss got him on loan, I think."

"Why does your boss need the extra muscle?"

"I'm not sure. Some new project he has going with some Middle Eastern group."

"Jihadis?"

"Uh-huh."

"What about Jacques Athos? You know him?"

"He's the boss's right hand."

"What's his real name?"

"I don't know."

Blunt cut in. "You don't know much, do you?"

"Only the boss or Athos or maybe Kowalski know the big picture. I just go where I'm told."

KD continued. "Who's Kowalski?"

"He runs Europe."

"So they sent you to Ireland?"

"I didn't say that. I'm on vacation. I don't know anything about those crates or what was in them."

"Do you know why Athos was in Lyon?"

"Don't know he was in Lyon."

Blunt frowned. "You don't remember me, do you?"

Creston stared at Blunt. "Wait a minute. Yeah, I remember you. It's been a long time. How was your friend's funeral? Heard it was closed casket."

Blunt took a step toward Creston and grabbed the front of his shirt. KD put her hand on Blunt's shoulder. "Let it go," she said. "He's going to prison for the rest of his life." She turned to Creston. "So you've got nothing else to say?"

"Nothing."

Blunt smiled. "Hope you wriggle out of your trouble here."

"Why's that?" Creston asked.

"Because I'd like to see the CIA get you."

AFTER THE IRISH police drove them back to the terminal, they found a coffee shop to sit in while the waited on their flight to Washington, DC.

"So Lysenko has dealings with a jihadi group," Blunt said.

"Makes sense. He's a black marketeer. What I'd like to know is if Colbert was working for Blaze or Lysenko when he killed Kalish and came after us."

"If he was working for Blaze, all this Lysenko stuff could just be a distraction."

"Exactly. We're disrupting Lysenko's plans, but it might have nothing to do with the hafnium."

"But even if he was working for Lysenko from the beginning, that's no guarantee that stealing the ore and working with jihadis is connected in any way. Could be different business deals."

"Could be. If we can turn up another lead, maybe we'll find out."

RODRIGUEZ LOOKED AT HER WATCH. She needed to get to her supply drop point. She walked by the church toward the foot trail up the west ridge. About an hour later, she came down a wooded hill onto an open field about one and a half miles from Agua Dulce. She slipped off her empty backpack and sat down in the weeds, waiting for her regular supply drop. She got her water at the village well, and she bought fresh food from the villagers, but for personal care supplies and CIA tech, she relied on a monthly parachute drop, which was why she was well away from the village.

She rubbed her neck and yawned. She was still sleeping in the bushes in her sleeping bag. Her one surveillance camera wasn't enough to make sure she would be safe in her cabin. And trying to shadow Gomez had been a waste of time. She never saw him do anything suspicious, and she couldn't watch him twenty-four seven anyway.

She heard the cargo plane and, looking up, saw the package attached to the parachute drifting down toward her location. When the package touched ground, she ran to it, pulled the parachute down, flattened it and rolled it, and then loaded her supplies into her backpack. All the usuals. MREs, tampons, more solar batteries, Chilean money. And three surveillance alarm kits.

She pulled on her backpack and started back toward the village. If anyone came up on her cabin in the middle of the night now, besides video, a blinding bright light would snap on and she'd hear beeping in her comms. Not perfect. Someone could still shoot into her cabin from a distance, but safe enough that she could sleep on the floor wearing her Kevlar vest. With any luck, one or two more weeks, one or two more village meetings, the US would win the mining contract, and she'd be out of here. She could put up with almost any inconvenience that long.

TWO DAYS LATER, Colbert was sitting on a sofa in a hotel suite in Rome. He'd taken the train from Barcelona to Marseille, then flown to Zurich and taken another train down to Rome. No one was following him. He tore the wrapper off a brand-new burner phone, activated it, and input the same number he'd called at the marina in Barcelona.

"Hello?"

"Colbert here. I'm in the clear."

"This a public phone?"

"No."

"Hold on."

A few minutes later, Lysenko came on the line. "Colbert, glad you escaped. Where are you?"

"Rome."

"I need you to come to Warsaw."

"Working for you seems problematic."

"We've still got you on loan from Blaze."

"That won't mean much if I'm dead."

"I don't think you have anything else to worry about."

"How did the Americans find me? I was clean when I landed in Paris."

"We think they found you on surveillance footage before you got to the safehouse."

"So they followed me down to Madrid?"

"That's what we think."

"Where are they now?"

"They've gone back to the US."

"I still need to be paid for the last job."

"That's Blaze's problem."

"They say it's yours."

"That shipment was lost."

"I wasn't working on consignment. I was straight salary. Plus I had a lot of expenses getting from there to here."

"Okay. We'll put the payment into your numbered account."

"Thanks. What's the new job?"

"Come to Warsaw and we'll talk about it."

"It better not be dodgy."

"It's straight up soldiering."

"Okay. I'll be on the first available flight."

In Washington, DC, KD and Frank were sitting at the dining room table near the kitchen island in her apartment. They were almost finished eating baked salmon with roasted potatoes and asparagus.

"You're a better cook than I remember," KD said.

"I think there's a compliment in there somewhere." Frank sipped his wine.

"You didn't cook that often."

"Cooked a lot while you were deployed."

"I never really thought about it. After I gave up running and gunning, while I was assigned to NASA, I cooked almost every night."

"I enjoyed it. Probably took it for granted."

"We took a lot of things for granted back then," KD said.

"How do you think things are going now?"

"Good. Really good. This question leading somewhere?"

"I'd like to see more of you."

"I'm in favor of that."

"And it doesn't look like you're planning to change jobs."

"I like what I do."

"And you changed up last time to be with me."

She nodded.

"So I was thinking maybe I should try to find a job up here," Frank said. "Then we could be together whenever you're not traveling."

"That's a big step."

"Yes, it is. I've got a lot of seniority right now. And my group does interesting work. No guarantee that I could find a job that would measure up in the DC area."

"But you've got a top security clearance. That counts for a lot around here."

"I haven't really started looking."

"And then we'd live together all the time?"

"That would be the idea."

KD took a swallow of wine. "When I said things are going great, I really meant it. And I really do want you up here."

"But?"

"I don't want you to take it the wrong way, but I think it would be better if you got your own apartment, at least for a little while."

"Because?"

"We've been seeing more and more of each other, but for me it's still sort of like a fantasy. When we're together, it's intense, then life goes back to being vanilla until the next time."

"That's why I want more."

"Me too. But real life, living every day, has to have more balance most of the time. It's not just twenty-four-hour intimacy. I love it, I want it, but real life is going on errands and figuring out who's doing which chore and making room for other relationships. I'm not saying that you're not my only one, I just saying that I need to go slow. I don't want to fall back into another version of what we had before. I want something better."

"I hear what you're saying."

"So if you want to move up here, that's a choice you're making for you, to see if we can keep going further. I love you, Frank, but I don't want you to feel like you've made a mistake if what we're doing now is the way our relationship stays."

Frank nodded. "Okay, Katie, I'm glad you're being so honest with me. I want the same thing as you. I want us to be married again and in tune with each other in a way we weren't before I screwed up. And I can understand your hesitancy. I'll just have to think through if this is the best time to take the leap."

"You do that." She set her cutlery down on her plate. "Are we done being serious?"

"We are."

"Good. I want to go back to focusing on this moment, feeling in love—"

He smiled. "Thinking about the make-up sex."

"Oh, you thought that was a fight?"

"My feelings are definitely hurt."

She laughed. "Think I should kiss your *owie*? Where is it?"

"Right here." He put a finger on his lips.

She drank off the last of her wine. "How many kisses do you think it might take?"

"I'll let you know when it's all better."

8

T he next morning, after KD and Blunt finished writing up their reports of their European trip, KD called Tina on the NDA office landline and put the phone on speaker. "Tina?"

"KD, what can I do for you?"

"Have you got any good news for us?"

"Nothing new. The Irish are keeping Creston locked up until his trial. Athos and Colbert haven't gone through any airport cameras that we're piggybacked on. Likewise Lysenko. And if they're flying private, we're not going to see them. Looks like Europe is a dead end for now."

Blunt cut in. "Any way to track Blaze Group?"

"None."

KD used her mouse to scroll back to the beginning of her report on her computer. "What's Davis up to?"

"Just looks like white nationalist, anti-immigrant activities. I was going to send the file over to the FBI," Tina replied.

"Could you send us the summary transcript first?"

"Sure, I'm emailing it now."

"Thanks, Tina." KD hung up the phone.

Blunt opened the summary transcript on his computer. "Fifty

pages. You're a glutton for punishment, Doc. This will take the rest of the day."

"Let's split it up so we get done sooner."

At 4:00 p.m., Blunt underlined a section of the transcript and then looked over to KD, sitting at her computer. "Doc, I might have something."

KD rolled her chair over to his desk and read the underlined section.

Davis: You go meet the guy. He has what you need.

Trevor: He's not a cop? You're sure?

Davis: I've worked with these people a long time. They're on the up and up.

Trevor: Okay then. Set up the meet.

KD turned to Blunt.

"I know it's thin, but it looks like they're talking about guns or explosives and Lysenko traffics in those," Blunt said.

"Could be drugs."

"Davis is not in drugs. His profile is all wrong."

"So you think this might be another angle to go after Lysenko?"

"I said it was thin, okay?"

She nodded. "This conversation was from—what? Six days ago. So either this Trevor guy has already picked up his shipment or he's about to. Let's have Tina find out who he is."

THE NEXT AFTERNOON, KD and Blunt were sitting in a Black Ford Explorer behind a state police SWAT team van on a gravel road in northern Virginia.

"Tina really came through," Blunt said.

"Yeah, it's got to be more than a coincidence that Trevor Billings and Chris Moore were both members of the White Riders prison gang and were both in prison at the same time."

"That his current location is a parole violation is a gift."

KD tapped the button on her comms headset. "Ready when you are, Lieutenant. Do everything you can to take him alive."

"Roger that."

The SWAT van took off down a long dirt driveway, KD and Blunt following close behind. Up ahead was a one-story clapboard house and a large, sheet metal pole barn. The SWAT van slid to a halt in front of the house and six SWAT team members jumped out of the back of the van. Four ran to the house, where the first officer yelled "Police" before the second and third officers battered the door open with a ram and they all ran inside.

The other two officers ran for the pole barn, where they kicked in a side door and disappeared into the building. KD and Blunt, wearing body armor, got out of their Explorer and hustled over to the barn. The two SWAT officers were standing by a tarp-covered pallet. Blunt unhooked the tiedowns on one side and lifted the tarp, exposing a stack of wooden crates.

"Assault rifles," Blunt said. "Still in their boxes."

The SWAT officers grinned.

"It's a definite win, guys," KD said.

They trotted back across the yard to the house, where the SWAT officers were filing out. "No one home," the lieutenant said.

"But the guns are in the barn, so they're coming back," KD said.

The lieutenant nodded. "I'll report in and see if the captain will approve a stakeout." He stepped away and made the phone call. After he finished the call and put his phone away, he came back to the group. "I've got the go-ahead."

"Good," KD replied.

"We'll hide the van behind the barn and set up down here."

"We'll drive back out and park in the bushes across the road," KD said. "When Billings drives in here, we'll come in behind him to block his escape."

"It's a plan."

"Let me fix the door," Blunt said. He pulled the forced-in door to the house back into place. "Now it doesn't look so obvious."

KD and Blunt drove back out to the highway and parked across the road on the shoulder behind a group of weedy saplings. "What do you think?" Blunt asked.

"Is this guy going to lead us anywhere? I don't know. But at least we're doing some good, so it's not a complete waste of time."

Blunt leaned his seat back. "May as well get comfortable."

Shortly after sundown, an old Ford Ranger truck flicked on its turn signal and started down Billings's dirt driveway.

"We're up." KD tapped her comms. "Coming to you."

She started the Explorer, crossed the road, and drove down the driveway with her headlights turned off, keeping well back and following the truck's taillights. When the truck pulled to a stop in front of the house, she stepped on the brake. A man got out of the driver's side of the truck. The SWAT team rushed him. KD flipped on her headlights and sped down the driveway until she skidded to a stop behind the Ford Ranger. The man was on the ground, face down, his hands cuffed behind him when KD and Blunt hopped out of their SUV. "Turn him over," KD said.

Two SWAT team members flipped him over. She looked at the man and at Billings's picture on her phone. "We got him. Great work. We'll take him from here."

"Don't forget our deal," the lieutenant said.

KD smiled. "No worries. You'll get him and the credit for the guns. We're not the FBI. We don't arrest people. That's why we brought you on board."

"I'm expecting to hear from you ASAP."

"And you will."

KD and Blunt loaded Billings into the back of their Explorer, his hands cuffed behind his back, and buckled his seatbelt.

"Where are you taking me?"

Blunt looked over his shoulder. "Just down to our man cave, woman cave, co-ed cave—what would you call it, Doc?"

"The cells."

THE NEXT MORNING, KD and Blunt went down to the cells in the basement of the NDA building. Billings was lying on a thin mattress on the flat steel cot hanging from the wall. They'd taken his belt, shoes, and personal effects the night before. The hallway outside the bars was empty, but the surveillance camera up near the ceiling was recording.

"Rise and shine," Blunt said. He shook the MacDonald's bag that he held in his hand.

KD unlocked the door. "Get up, Trevor."

Billings rolled off the cot and stood up. "What about my shoes?"

"Later."

They took him to an interview room at the end of the hall. Steel table with a steel chair bolted to the floor on one side, two office chairs on the other side, live camera in the corner at the ceiling by the door.

"Sit down," KD said.

Billings sat down. Blunt slid the MacDonald's bag across the table. Billings opened the bag and took out a sausage egg biscuit, a hash brown, and a coffee. "Thanks," he said.

"More than you deserve," Blunt replied.

KD and Blunt waited until Billings was almost done with his breakfast. "You're in a world of hurt," Blunt said. "Cases of automatic rifles. No permits. That's real time in a maximum security prison."

Trevor spoke with his mouth full. "Is that supposed to scare me?"

"Some prisons are mainly white gangs. Some prisons are mainly black gangs. Keeps them from beefing with each other so much. Where would you like to go?"

"Home. I heard you talking to that trooper. You're not cops. You've got no right to hold me."

KD shook her head. "Who did you buy the guns from?"

"What guns? I don't know anything about any guns."

"That's your story?"

"Yep."

"Maybe you can work that story with the state of Virginia, I don't care one way or another. But if you don't tell us who you bought the guns from, we're going to tell your friends that you cooperated because you were afraid of my partner. He can be intimidating."

"Especially to racists," Blunt added.

KD continued. "We're going to spread the word that you're a snitch, that you bought the guns as part of a sting, that you're turning on everyone now that the operation is over."

"No one will believe you."

"You're going into the general population at that new county jail where they take the prison overflow. How many high school dropouts have to be suspicious before you get shanked?"

"You can't do that."

"Sure we can," Blunt said.

KD leaned forward. "Or you can tell us the name of the seller and how you communicated. We give you back to the troopers. No one knows you ever spoke with us. Maybe your lawyer can make the charges disappear. Do yourself a solid."

Billings pushed the food wrappers out of the way and sipped his coffee. Blunt tapped his fingers on the table. "Tick tock."

"I'm thinking."

"What's there to think about? This is a one-time offer. The next deal will be worse," KD said.

"No one will know?"

"We won't tell. We're after these people because they're terrorists. We don't care about your court case."

"Terrorists? You mean like foreigners?"

"Exactly."

"You give me your word?"

"Yes."

Billings was quiet for a moment. "The guy I dealt with was named Solomon Greer. He looked like a white guy. Maybe Greek or something. Had a white moustache and bushy eyebrows."

"He was the guy Davis put you in touch with?" KD asked.

"Davis. How do you know about him?"

"That's our job."

"Yeah, he's the guy Davis sent me to. Met him at the Chicken Shack just south of Arlington, Virginia. He gave me a burner."

"Do you still have the phone?"

"No. Tossed it."

"Where?"

"Down a storm sewer on Military Drive."

"In Arlington?"

"Out past Reston."

"How did you deal with the guns?"

"I left the cash in a suitcase in a dumpster behind a restaurant."

"In Reston."

"Yeah. The guns were in a semi-truck parked in an old Kmart parking lot."

"No cameras?"

"No cameras."

"You trusted him to come through?"

"Davis said he was the real deal. I trusted Davis."

KD glanced at Blunt. "We'll be back."

They went out into the hall. KD took out her smartphone and put it on speaker. "Did you get all of that, Tina?"

"Yeah."

"Think the phone will be of any use?"

"It hasn't rained."

"Send some people to find it."

They went back into the interview room. "If your information checks out for us, we're good."

"You won't tell?"

"We won't tell. We're turning you over to the Virginia troopers. If we have any more questions, we'll be in touch."

THE NEXT AFTERNOON, KD got a call from Tina. She put it on speaker. "Solomon Greer is an alias. No record in the crime database. Closest real person owns a drycleaner in Charleston, West Virginia. Skinny, dark-haired guy who's lived there forty years."

"No surprise there. What about the phone?"

"Phone was a little wonky, but we managed to scrape it. Found the phone number that had called. Traced it back to an address in

Arlington. The owners are Sam and Thelma Regent. They bought the house five years ago."

"Do the Regents live there or are they renting it out?"

"Don't know."

"Can you email the report?"

"Sending it now." Tina ended the call.

At 4:00 p.m., KD and Blunt drove out to the address in the Dominion Hills neighborhood in Arlington and parked on the street within sight of a two-story brick house with a wrap-around porch.

"That's our target?" KD asked.

"Yes, looks like it belongs in Mr. Roger's Neighborhood, doesn't it?"

At 5:30 p.m., a blue Volvo pulled up in the driveway, and a white-haired man with a huge mustache got out of the car and started into the house.

"Looks like our guy," KD said.

Blunt took three photos on a digital camera and emailed them to Tina. Then he sent a text: *Please print the photos.* "Think he's coming back out?"

"I hope so. I'd like to look inside."

At 7:00 p.m., the man came out of the house, got in the car, and drove away. KD called Tina. "Tell me you're up on his phone."

"Sorry, couldn't triangulate it from the cell tower."

"We'll just have to be quick."

They drove up into the white-haired man's driveway and walked up the sidewalk as if they were expected. Blunt rang the doorbell. No answer. He banged on the door. Nothing. He got out his lock picks. As he was about to insert the pick, the door started to open. He folded the tool into his hand.

An older woman wearing designer workout clothes stood in the doorway. "Yes?"

KD smiled. "Sorry to bother you in the evening, but is this the Regent residence?"

She shook her head.

"We're trying to get in touch with Sam Regent. It's quite important."

"Well, he doesn't live here."

"Really? I guess we must have the wrong information. Sorry to bother you."

They got into their SUV and backed down the driveway.

"She lied to us," Blunt said. "So she's in on it."

"Maybe. Maybe she's just suspicious of strangers. Maybe they're renting through an agency and don't know the owners."

"Doesn't mean they're not our targets."

"Let's see what Billings has to say."

The next morning, they went to the Fairfax County Detention Center in Fairfax, Virginia, parked in the visitor parking, and went in through the security screening, where a deputy met them and ushered them to an interview room where Billings was waiting.

"You two," Billings said.

"We need for you to identify a man from a photo lineup," KD said.

Blunt laid five photos down on the table in front of Billings. Each photo contained the picture of a man with a white mustache walking up a driveway. Billings pushed each of them out of the way after he looked at them until he came to the fourth photo, which was the man Blunt had photographed in Arlington. "That's Solomon Greer."

"You sure?" Blunt asked.

"That's him. No doubt."

"Did you ever see him with anyone?"

"No, only met him the once."

"But you know for a fact that's him."

"Absolutely."

"Thanks for your cooperation."

KD and Blunt went back out to their Explorer. KD called Tina. "Billings identified our target as Greer. Can you get a stingray up on the Dominion Hills house?"

"It'll be up by the end of day."

"And wiretaps, if they have a landline."

"No problem."

"And we want to know everything there is to know about Sam and Thelma Regent."

9

Meanwhile, forty fighters from the New Islamic Caliphate's Chilean and Bolivian drug smuggling operation were massed in a mountain valley two miles west of Agua Dulce. At dusk Commander Bashir drove into the tent encampment in a Range Rover with a guide and two mining engineers. Saad waved at him and started across the encampment to meet him.

"You have done well," Bashir said.

"Thank you, Commander. The men are eager."

Bashir unfolded a map on the hood of the Range Rover and illuminated it with a penlight. "We're going to take the most direct route to Agua Dulce. We'll drive straight through the village, up the hill to the temple, and set up a fenced perimeter. Then our engineers will assess how to begin the mining operation. We'll ignore the villagers unless they make trouble."

"When do we leave?"

"First light."

"I don't think we can tear down this camp that quickly."

"Then we leave it. We'll come back and tear it down later. We have plenty of supplies. We need to move quickly to secure the mine."

As the sun was coming over the eastern mountains, they formed a convoy of trucks—fighters in the first trucks, followed by truckloads of supplies to set up camp—and drove up the valley and over the pass, coming down the rocky switchbacks through the scrub grass and thorny shrubs and through the next valley to Agua Dulce. As they drove up the main street, the fighters brandishing their AK-47s, some of the villagers ran into their houses while others disappeared into the surrounding woods. The jihadis turned right at the plaza in front of the church, drove past the end of the cross street and up the hill to the temple ruins.

Saad jumped out of the Range Rover and walked off the perimeter for their encampment. The north side was protected by a sheer cliff dropping almost one hundred feet and the west side beyond the temple ruin was protected by a series of huge rocks too difficult to climb without equipment, so he directed fighters to dig two machine gun emplacements, the first facing the main path up from the village, the second at the open southeast corner. Other fighters carried steel fence posts and chain-link fencing from the back of a flatbed truck to start on the perimeter fence. When he was satisfied that the work was going as planned, he picked out two fighters. "You two. Go find the American and bring her here."

Meanwhile, Bashir and the mining engineers had gone into the temple antechamber, turned on the lights that Rodriguez has set up, found the mining tunnel, and made their way down the shaft.

They shined their flashlights on the mine face. Zircon crystals twinkled on the surface of the surrounding silicate ore. Bashir smiled. It looked even more promising than he had been led to believe. He turned to the engineers. "What do you think?"

One of the engineers tapped at the mine face with a rock hammer. "Power tools will make short work of it," he said.

The second engineer nodded. "We'll build a track back to the entrance and out into the encampment, then we'll be able to move cartloads of material."

The first one studied the roof with his flashlight. "We'll need to install a roof bolt system first."

"Commander!" Saad called down the shaft.

Bashir came out of the mine and followed Saad out of the temple. Gomez stood between two armed fighters, a deep frown on his face. "What are you doing here? This isn't what we agreed. You gave me your word."

"Our plans have changed," Bashir said. "Don't worry, you'll be paid."

"It's not about the money."

"Then what is it about? You get paid now instead of later. You can leave whenever you like. You weren't planning on staying for the mining, no matter who got the contract, were you?"

"But now everyone will know I told you where the mine was."

"They were always going to find out eventually."

"But you gave me your word."

"Enough. Tomas Sinchi and Roberto Cuzco represent the two main factions of villagers, correct? Bring them here so we can discuss our payment arrangements." He turned to the fighters. "Escort Gomez down the hill and bring up Sinchi and Cuzco when they appear."

The fighters led Gomez down the hill. Then he walked down the cross street to the plaza in front of the abandoned church. Groups of villagers had gathered, talking among themselves. Gomez found Tomas and his family. "Tomas, I must speak to you."

Tomas eyed him suspiciously. "Why were you up at the temple?"

"This wasn't supposed to happen. I was just trying to give us more options for choosing who would do the mining. Make sure our people got the best deal."

"So these are your Muslim friends, the ones who are supposed to respect our traditions?"

"I was tricked."

"But you told them where the mine was."

"I was foolish. I admit it."

"Your apology makes no difference now."

"They want to meet you and Roberto to discuss payment arrangements."

"I cannot meet with anyone unless the village agrees."

"Then call a meeting. We're all here."

MEANWHILE, Rodriguez was lying in the weeds near the path that ran between the village and her cabin. She'd run out of the village when she saw the truck convoy and had taken a roundabout path back toward her cabin to get her go-bag. She peeked down the hill. No one was on the path, and she couldn't see any of the trucks, which meant these invaders probably knew where the mine was. She turned and crept up the path, her pistol down at her side, but as she came to the crest of the hill, she saw two armed men, Middle Easterners dressed in military clothes, standing guard at her cabin. She couldn't risk a gunfight. She wasn't going to be able to get her gear or her satellite phone, at least not now.

She veered off to her right, staying in the bushes, and made her way to a spot overlooking the village on the opposite side from the ruins. She lay down in the brush, got out her binoculars, and watched the activity over at the temple ruin. Middle Eastern men were unloading machinery, rolling out chain-link fencing to build a perimeter, and setting up tents. Who the hell were they? She looked down into the plaza in front of the church. It looked like the villagers were holding a meeting. She hoped they would deal, and not resist, at least for the time being. She didn't want any of them to get hurt.

THE VILLAGERS GATHERED in the plaza to discuss their options, women as well as men. They knew that they were outgunned and that there was no hope of Chilean or Bolivian soldiers coming to their aid, at least not in the short term, so they finally agreed to send Tomas and Roberto as their representatives. Gomez led them up the hill to the jihadi encampment.

"So you've been working for the Muslims," Roberto said.

"I was just trying to get us the best deal," Gomez said. "The Americans can't be trusted."

"You told them where the mine was. Admit it."

"They lied to me."

"Once they knew," Tomas said, "there was no reason for them to hold back."

"I hope whatever they paid you was worth it," Roberto said.

"I wasn't the only one bargaining with outsiders," Gomez replied.

"But you were the only one giving up our secrets."

Bashir and Saad were waiting for them on the steps of the temple. Gomez spoke in Spanish. "This is Commander Bashir of the New Islamic Caliphate."

"I'm glad you made the right choice," Bashir said.

"You're a long way from home," Roberto said. "Isn't your caliphate in the Middle East?"

"We have interests everywhere. We don't want to harm you. We're here because we're going to mine this ore."

"The temple is a sacred place," Tomas said. "It must not be vandalized, and we need to be able to come here to seek guidance from the spirits."

"We will take every possible precaution," Bashir replied.

"But will that be good enough?" Tomas asked.

"And can we take your word? You already broke your word with Gomez," Roberto said.

"We want to treat you fairly," Bashir replied. "We'll do the mining, and we'll give you one-third of the profits. And if any of your people want jobs, they will be paid wages besides. Once you prove that you won't interfere with our work, we'll allow you to come to the temple for religious purposes."

"I don't know if the village will agree," Tomas said.

"We have possession of the site, and we have the guns. Make sure that your people see reason."

Roberto, Tomas, and Gomez left. Saad turned to Bashir. "They're lucky we don't destroy their infidel temple. Are you really going to let them come up here to worship?"

"No. After the rest of our men arrive with the heavy mining equipment, and we have the mining underway, they'll start spending their money and forget all about their pretend religion. But enough about that. How are our security preparations going?"

"We've almost got the fencing and the machine gun placements completed."

"What about our far perimeter?"

"Scouts are watching the trails approaching the village. No one will get close without us knowing about it."

"Thank you, Saad."

Bashir went back into the temple, where the engineers were in the antechamber discussing the best place to create a larger entrance that would lead directly to the mine.

"If we move this stone table," the first engineer said, "we could merely enlarge the current doorway and run the track straight down to the mine."

"We could dig a new shaft," the second engineer said. "Come in through the side of the temple and leave this room undisturbed."

"Those are the two best options?" Bashir asked.

The engineers nodded.

"I assume digging a new shaft will take more time?"

"That's the price for protecting the site," the second engineer replied.

"There's nothing particularly special about this site," Bashir said. "It looks just like all the others up and down the Andes. Move the table and go out the front."

Bashir left the antechamber and walked out into the middle of the compound. Fighters were putting up the last section of chain-link fence, and the machine guns were in place at the gate and the southeast corner. Their trucks were lined up in the middle of the compound and men were putting up a row of tents between the trucks and the sheer cliff on the back side of the ruins. He got out his satellite phone and texted the Caliphate Council to update them on their progress.

Allah be praised, came the reply. *We will not forget what you have done.*

BACK AT NDA HEADQUARTERS, KD and Blunt were at their desks when Tina called. KD put the phone on speaker.

"Hey, guys, there's nothing on the Regents. Their records are clean."

"Clean? That's hard to believe," KD said.

"If we hadn't scraped the phone we retrieved from the storm drain, we wouldn't know anything. And the house isn't a rental, so Greer is probably Regent."

"So it's all a big goose egg?" Blunt asked.

"The only thing of interest is a new burner phone. Sam Regent called a landline phone in Prague, Czech Republic. The phone is at the offices of SunBright Technologies, which is a cover business for the Blaze Group. So maybe it's something or maybe it's not. You want me to risk digging in Prague?"

"No," KD said. "I don't think this is going to lead to anything specific enough to act on. Thanks for going the extra mile."

"You bet."

KD ended the call and swiveled her desk chair to face Blunt. "So it looks like Colbert was working for Blaze when he came after us."

"Which means Blaze were probably the ones that were after the CIA's ore sample."

"So that's the end of it."

"Unless we get a new lead off of Davis."

"Do you really think that's going to happen?"

"I don't know."

AT DUSK, Gomez went to Tomas and Maria's clay brick house to try to explain himself and win them over. As he walked down the main street, neighbors who were still out in their yards were watching him, but no one raised a hand or called out a hello. They thought he was a traitor. But he wasn't. He really had only wanted what was best for the village, and why shouldn't he be paid for his work if no one was harmed? Even now, the only ones to suffer were Rodriguez and her American consortium. Why should anyone care about them?

He knocked on Tomas and Maria's door. Tomas came to the door, but he didn't invite him in. Instead, he come out onto the stoop and shut the door behind him.

"You're not welcome here."

"Cousin, I was only trying to help our people get the best deal. Truly. I was just leveling the playing field. I didn't tell Bashir anything that the Americans didn't already know."

"Did the Americans act on the knowledge they had? Did they take over our temple and push us out of the way?"

"Bashir lied to me, and I accept responsibility for that mistake. I know better now. I know that no outsiders can be trusted."

"But how will you prove that *you* can be trusted?"

"This incident will seem like a bump in the road once the money from the mining starts flowing."

"What happens when Chile and Bolivia come to an agreement? Will we get anything? What happens if the Muslims coming causes Chile and Bolivia to work out their differences more quickly?"

"Our time to benefit from the mine was always going to be short."

"Don't come here again." Tomas went inside and shut the door.

Gomez headed back down the street toward his house. If Tomas wouldn't listen, then he didn't stand a chance with the other villagers. Originally, he'd planned to stay in Agua Dulce long enough so that he wouldn't be suspected of helping Bashir, but now he might as well leave as soon as possible. He walked past his house, took the cross street, and went up the hill to the brightly lit temple compound. A guard stood at the closed gate. Gomez spoke in Spanish. "I'm here to see Commander Bashir."

The guard nodded, and then yelled to someone in the distance in a language Gomez didn't know. Someone yelled back to the guard. He opened the gate. Another fighter escorted Gomez across the encampment to Bashir's tent.

Bashir looked up from his laptop computer. "So, why are you here?"

"Did you find the mine?"

"Yes, I did. It was where you said it was."

"Then I'm here for the payment you promised."

"The double payment?"

"That's correct."

Bashir smiled. "So you've decided you're not too angry with me to demand your money."

"I only want what you promised."

"And you'll have it. But I'm a little busy right now. I'll deposit the money in your account as soon as I have the time."

"But you swore to pay me."

"And I will."

"I can't stay here. The villagers have turned against me."

"That's not my problem. You chose your side. I'll pay you when I have the time."

"But I need my money now."

Bashir stood up. "Enough. I'll pay you when I'm ready. Goodbye."

Bashir called to the fighter who was waiting outside the tent. He led Gomez back across the compound to the gate. Gomez started back down the hill to the village, walking slowly to let his eyes adjust to the dark. Was Bashir going to pay him? Or had he misjudged him all along? His entire future depended upon that payment, a payment he'd earned by alienating his kin. He couldn't force Bashir to pay him. He had no leverage since he'd already given up the location of the mine.

Surely Bashir was just toying with him, proving he had all the power. He'd always kept his word before. So he was just going to have to stay out of Bashir's way, let him take his time, keep checking his bank account, and keep providing information until the payment cleared, no matter how much the villagers shunned him.

. . .

AFTER GOMEZ MADE his way down the middle of the street past Roberto and Anna's house, Roberto came out into his yard with the satellite phone Juan Carlos had given him and called the number in the address book.

"Who's calling?" a voice asked in Spanish.

"Juan Carlos gave me this phone."

"You must be Roberto. I'm Lysenko. I'm the one who Juan Carlos reports to. Do you have information?"

"Is my deal the same?"

"Of course."

"The New Islamic Caliphate has taken over the mine."

"When?"

"Today."

"When will they start mining?"

"I'm not sure. Villagers aren't allowed up at the temple. They're building a camp and unloading equipment."

"So the mine is at the temple."

Roberto looked up at the security lights shining out from the compound surrounding the temple. What he said made no difference now. "Yes, the entrance to the mine is in the antechamber of the temple."

"Your payment will be in your bank account tomorrow. If anything changes, call back. If your information is useful, you'll receive another payment."

Roberto went inside his house. Anna was washing the last of the supper dishes. "Well?"

"I spoke with Juan Carlos's friend Lysenko. The money should be in our bank account tomorrow. We can use the sat phone to find out if it's really there."

She turned from the sink and dried her hands. "When are we leaving?"

"Lysenko will pay for more information. I think we should wait a few more days just in case we find out something that could get us another payment. When we have all the money, then we can arrange for the tourist visas and airline tickets."

"It's finally going to happen."

"It is."

She came to him and took his hands in hers. "Promise me you won't turn into Gomez and sell out our people."

"I've only spoken the truth, and we've only been paid for telling the truth. I haven't revealed any secrets or worked against our people in any way."

"Gomez might have thought the same thing."

"But he told them where the mine was."

"And maybe they promised him they would negotiate in good faith."

"I'm not Gomez."

"No, you're not. I'm just saying we need to be careful."

10

The next day, a three-man scouting team from Lysenko's group parachuted onto a smugglers' airstrip cut into the woods near the Bolivian-Chilean border and were met by a Chilean woman driving a Jeep. The men slung their backpacks into the back of the Jeep and climbed in. The woman turned the Jeep in a tight circle and started back the way she had come, driving down a dirt track through the tall weeds. Then she turned right off the track onto a two-lane, gravel road that led to the mountains in the distance.

Four hours later, as the light was falling behind the near mountains, they came to a stop before the last switchback up the mountain. The scouting team got out of the Jeep, slipped by the sentry watching the road, and crept up a hill where they had a good view of the village down below and the temple ruins beyond. The Caliphate fighters had set up a fenced perimeter around the ruins and were carrying equipment into the temple. Down in the village, they strolled among the villagers, their automatic rifles slung over their shoulders. The scouts watched until the valley was completely dark. Then they slipped back down the hill, hurried back to the Jeep, and drove back to the airstrip, where the woman left them.

. . .

WHILE THE SCOUTS were surveilling the village, Rodriguez, sneaking down a meandering trail to the east of the village, saw a glint of reflection on the opposite hill. She took out her binoculars, spotted the scouts, lay down under cover of some bushes, and kept watch on them. When the scouts crawled away, she moved up the slope toward the gravel road that switchbacked down the back of the mountain, keeping to the bushes on the side of the trail, but the scouts had disappeared.

Who were they? They weren't with the Middle Easterners, that was for sure. And they weren't CIA, or they would have been trying to contact her. What did she know? The Middle Easterners had taken the mine. It looked like they were making preparations to start mining as soon as possible. The villagers had been overrun; they hadn't ceded the mine willingly. Now there were new players. Trouble was brewing.

She made her way back around to her cabin. A man was still posted at the door. She needed her satellite phone and her go-bag, but she couldn't risk alerting the rest of the Middle Easterners. Right now, her anonymity was her biggest strength. Where could she get a phone? The villagers had been ostracizing Gomez ever since the Middle Easterners had shown up. They must have thought he was involved. Is that why he tried to kill her? Did he have a satellite phone? Could she find it and call for backup?

Later, while the villagers were meeting at the plaza, Rodriguez picked the lock on the back door to Gomez's one-room house and crept into the dark. She turned on her flashlight. In the kitchen area, she rummaged through the cupboards, took a few sweet potatoes and several pieces of flat bread, and then moved through to the living area. Where would Gomez keep a satellite phone? Not where anyone could see it, and not outside where it might be found by playing children. She moved to the bedroom area. A narrow bed, a simple night table, some folded clothes on two open shelves. She looked under the bed, then gently lifted the straw mattress. Nothing. The sat phone must be in a hidey-hole, if it existed at all. She couldn't risk staying here any longer. Well, at least she'd managed to scrounge some food.

She made her way toward the plaza, staying in the shadows, on the lookout for any Middle Easterners. She got close enough the see the villagers gathered, both the men and the women, torches illuminating the scene, which meant a meeting of the most important sort, but she couldn't get close enough to hear what they were saying. She worked her way up the hillside, over the ridge, and down the other side to a depression hidden by bushes on all sides. The blanket she'd scrounged yesterday was still there. She hated stealing from the villagers, but she didn't have a choice. She had to stay hidden, had to stay warm, had to eat, if she were going to make a difference. She needed a satellite phone. That was the only way she was going to get help.

THE NEXT MORNING, four cargo planes landed and took off at the smugglers' airstrip, one after the other, until twenty-nine mercenaries from Lysenko's Ciudad del Este compound, their gear, and four Humvees had been unloaded. All the men wore camouflage clothes and body armor and were armed with Glock pistols and automatic rifles.

After the first plane landed, Patrick Colbert got off, spotted the scouts waiting at the side of the airstrip, ushered them under the shade of a tree, and debriefed them. They gave him a topographical map where they'd marked out the main footpaths, the two streets, the abandoned church, and the temple compound.

"How many jihadis?"

The lead scout spoke. "We're not sure. We counted thirty-four at the compound, but there could be more."

"Were the villagers helping them?"

"No."

"But they're completely dug in? Security fence, fifty caliber machine guns, and trenches?"

"Yes."

"You three are riding with me."

They stood under the tree, waiting as each plane landed,

unloaded its soldiers, supplies, and a Humvee, and took off. Finally, Colbert stood on a wooden crate and called the mercenaries together. "You were all briefed last night. You know the mission. This will be a hard day. If everyone does their job, by nightfall we'll be in control of the mine, and we'll all receive our bonuses. Do not accidentally shoot the locals. Jihadis only. We want cooperation, not resistance. Any questions?"

The men murmured and shook their heads.

"Let's go."

They crowded into the Humvees and drove off down the dirt track toward the two-lane gravel road. In the distance, they could see the arid mountains. They passed by a woman herding goats, two boys carrying buckets of water, and a family of five riding in a rusty pickup truck. But no jihadis. On the incline before they came to the switch-backs up the mountain, Colbert stopped the caravan. He turned to his tech specialist. "Send up a drone."

The tech specialist got the drone out of its box, tested the camera, and sent it flying. Using a small tablet, he sent it zigzagging up the switchbacks, searching for fighters or roadblocks, but the road seemed clear all the way to the village. Colbert stood beside the tech specialist and watched the drone's progress on the tablet. "Nothing. Hard to believe they're not expecting trouble. Bring it back."

The tech specialist collected the drone, and they started up the switchbacks. As the first Humvee made its way up the rocky trail through the spindly trees and came to the first hard right turn, its front end exploded. It caught fire and fell sideways across the road. Gunfire peppered in from uphill. The other Humvees screeched to a halt, the men rushing out to provide cover fire for the men in the wrecked Humvee. Teams of two crouched down behind boulders or behind trees, firing uphill, looking for targets, but the jihadis were all but invisible. Five men from the burning Humvee lay dead in the road, the remaining three trapped behind the rear of the truck.

Two teams moved up on either side of the road, scrambling from rock to rock, until they were close enough to draw the fire away from the trapped men. The men ran for it. One was shot in the leg and dragged down the road to safety by the other two. As the two teams retreated behind them, one of the team members was shot in the head and carried back by the others.

Colbert spoke over his comms. "Regroup in the valley."

The three Humvees slowly backed down the mountain, the mercenaries firing uphill as they retreated. It was dark by the time they were back down in the valley and out of range of gunfire.

Colbert gathered his lieutenants. "What a shitshow. They were dug in like ticks."

"We didn't see them from the drone," the tech specialist said.

"But they're moving around now," Colbert replied. "Send the drone back up so we can find out how many we're up against."

"It's too dark. The drone will pick up heat signatures, but that won't be precise enough to give us a firm number."

"We'll set up camp here. I'll call the boss. He should be in Ciudad del Este by now."

WHEN THE FIRING STARTED, Rodriguez made her way to a spot along a ridge where she could see the burning truck and the Middle Easterners firing from their hidden positions. Most, if not all, of the Middle Easterners were engaged in the battle. She rushed back toward the village, lay down in a spot where she had a good view of the main street, and watched. The villagers were milling about, obviously worried about the fighting, but there were no Middle Easterners in sight. She got out her binoculars. Two men stood guard at the gate to the perimeter fence around the temple compound. She hurried down a narrow trail toward her cabin. No one was guarding the door.

She scampered across the open ground to her cabin door and pushed it open. Her supplies and her clothes were strewn around the floor. Her laptop computer and her automatic rifle were missing. Her cot lay on its side. She glanced out the door. No one. She pushed the cot out of the way and lifted a floorboard. Her go-bag was still there, lying on the dirt. She pulled it out and unzipped it. Her satellite phone, MRE rations, another pistol, and several full pistol magazines were all there.

She zipped it closed and ran full speed for the cover of the trees and high grass. Then she made her way over the ridge and down into the next valley, eating a MRE protein bar as she walked. After she'd gone a few miles, she sat down against a tree and turned on her satellite phone. The battery still had power. She input the emergency number for the CIA control desk and gave them her code.

"What's your emergency?"

"My position has been overrun. Two groups are fighting over the mine, a Middle Eastern group and another group. Need immediate support."

"I'll relay your message."

COMMANDER BASHIR DROVE through the village and past Rodriguez's cabin to the start of the gravel road down the mountain. He climbed out of his Range Rover and got out his binoculars to watch the last of their enemies retreating down the bottom switchback. Saad came up the road toward him. "They're on the run."

Bashir stopped looking through the binoculars. "They're not done."

"They lost a Humvee and five men."

"How many have we lost?"

"Only two men wounded."

"They'll try again tomorrow."

"We have the high ground, and there is only one way up on this side of the mountain."

"So there'll be hard fighting tomorrow."

"Should we booby trap the mine just in case?"

"No, we can't risk the mine being buried in a cave-in. We need to be mining as soon as possible."

"There's a natural choke point at the end of the last switchback. We'll set a trap there."

"Very good."

"Will you inform the Caliphate of our situation?"

"What can they do? Better to wait until we've crushed these infidels. Then our success will seem all the more complete."

THE NEXT MORNING, Lysenko landed at the smugglers' air strip with reinforcements. He contacted Colbert by satellite phone. "What did the drone tell us?"

"They're dug in at the end of the last switchback, and they've hardened the perimeter to their compound surrounding the temple."

"We're on our way. I've brought twelve more soldiers and an armored personnel carrier with a fifty-caliber machine gun, so we won't have any trouble on the mountain this time."

By early afternoon they were on the switchbacks going up the mountain. The armored personnel carrier pushed the wrecked Humvee off the road and continued on, the other Humvees following. The jihadis had mined the road at the third switchback, but it made no difference to the armored personnel carrier. It bounced back and forth as it set off the mine, rolled backward a few feet, and then continued up the mountain, bullets bouncing off its armor. At the last switchback, the armored personnel carrier opened up with its machine gun and punched through the jihadis' ambush. Lysenko's mercenaries jumped out of their Humvees and rushed up the hill in the armored personnel carrier's wake, scattering the jihadis into a disorderly retreat.

Lysenko's forces stopped to regroup at the top of the ridge. The drone showed the villagers in a panic, men grabbing their hunting rifles and then running off into the woods with the woman and children, and the jihadis hustling through the village and back to their camp at the temple.

As the armored personnel carrier, flanked by mercenaries on both sides, started down the path from Rodriguez's cabin to the village, Lysenko's men rounded up as many villagers as they could, disarming the men and locking them all in the dilapidated church.

Lysenko pointed to two of his fighters. "You two guard the church. The rest of us will take the jihadi compound."

Lysenko's mercenaries went up the path to the ruins, the armored personnel carrier in front, but there was no return fire. When they got to the temple compound, the jihadis were gone.

Lysenko turned to Colbert. "Secure the area and sweep for explosives."

Lysenko went into the temple. Colbert directed men to search the compound and the village and to set up a perimeter controlling the roads and trails into the village. When he was done, he found Lysenko at the mine face. "What do you want to do about the villagers?"

"If we're going to have any semblance of legality, we need them alive and cooperative, so we've got to get them all to come back and be part of the deal we're going to make. Use the PA on one of the Humvees to broadcast a message into the surrounding countryside."

Over the next few hours, some villagers trickled back into the village, where they were put into the church with the others. Lysenko's men provided MREs and water. Finally, when he thought most of the villagers were assembled, Lysenko strode up to the altar of the church, flanked by two men carrying assault rifles.

"Good afternoon," he said in Spanish. "We don't have any disagreement with you. We want you to be safe and to fully benefit from the ore on your land. Promise not to fight us and you can go about your business."

Tomas stepped into the aisle. "We do not want trouble. We will not fight you."

"Are you the head man here?" Lysenko asked.

"I am one of the elders," Tomas replied.

"Is everyone here?"

"Most, but not everyone."

"Where would they go?"

Tomas shrugged. "Into the woods."

"Where is the American geologist?"

"Senora Rodriguez? We don't know. No one has seen her since the Muslims arrived."

"Is she dead?"

"We don't know."

"Did you sign a contract with the jihadis?"

"They made an offer, but it was not up to us."

"You're going to sign a contract with us to mine the ore. Your village will make a lot of money."

"Why should we trust you? You've taken the mine by force. You're holding us against our will."

"We're just holding you for your own protection until the fighting is over."

"We can leave?"

"Are these your family?" He pointed to Tomas's son and granddaughter.

Tomas nodded.

"We'll keep these two in custody for the time being. The rest of you can go."

"Why? Why are you holding them?"

"To make sure you'll cooperate. You decide to sign the mining contract, and we'll let them go."

The villagers filed out of the church.

Lysenko turned to his men. "Take these two to our camp."

"Don't worry, father," Tomas's son said. "We'll be all right."

Lysenko and his bodyguards drove back up to the compound, where guards let them in the gate. Lysenko spotted Colbert directing two men unloading a truck and went over to him. "What's our situation?"

"Three wounded, two dead. So we're down to thirty-three soldiers."

"What have you found here?"

"The jihadis brought a lot of good equipment, but not enough to start mining. They must have more equipment and personnel on the way. And you're going to need about double the men to hold the mine indefinitely, plus the miners and engineers to operate it."

"The lead engineers will be arriving by helicopter tomorrow. As soon as they've made their assessment, the workers and equipment will be trucked in."

"What about more soldiers?"

"I've got a dozen on standby."

"We need them now. And more ammunition and a case of rocket-propelled grenades with launchers, just in case."

"Okay, we'll fly them in first thing in the morning. So far as tonight, everyone stands watch on four-hour shifts."

Lysenko went into Bashir's tent, sat on Bashir's cot, and used his satellite phone to call his offices in Ciudad del Este to make arrangements for the engineers, soldiers, and weapons. Most of the villagers had come back, but he had to make sure that the ones who were missing weren't working against him or communicating with other villages. He called Juan Carlos.

"Mr. Lysenko. I hadn't expected to hear from you."

"Where are you?"

"I'm on my rounds. I'm about twenty miles west of Agua Dulce."

"I'm in control of the mine, but some of the villagers have left. Can you find them and convince them that it's safe to come back?"

"Is it safe?"

"Yes. My people won't harm them."

"But is the fighting done?"

"Maybe. It's not clear. But the stronger my position is, the safer it's going to be. That's why I need the villagers to return to the village. We need their consent for the mining contract."

"Okay, I know some secluded areas where someone might go for safety. I'll have a look."

RODRIGUEZ WAS WALKING in the dark along a foot path to the west of Agua Dulce when she saw light in the distance. She crept toward it, moving slowly and carefully so as not to be heard. As she neared, she saw Roberto, Anna, their children, and three more families all sitting around a fire near a rock outcropping where water trickled from the rocks to a pond. She circled them to make sure they were alone before she approached the fire.

"Don't be alarmed," she said in Spanish.

"Cora." Roberto stood. "We thought you had left."

"Or that you were dead," Anna added.

Roberto and Anna came to her and hugged her.

"I managed to avoid the Middle Easterners," Rodriguez replied, "and I got my gear while they were fighting the other group. Do you know who these groups are?"

"The Muslims are with the New Islamic Caliphate," Roberto said. "The other group work for a man called Lysenko. They've chased off the Caliphate for now. They're camped in the next valley."

"Come, sit," Anna said.

Rodriguez squatted near the fire. "The Muslims aren't done fighting. I guess both sides are after the ore?"

Roberto nodded. "The Caliphate made a good offer. They do the work, and the village gets one-third of the profit."

"And Lysenko?"

"We don't know. We ran when the fighting got to the village."

"And you haven't gone back?"

"We're waiting to see what happens first."

"Good plan."

"What are you going to do?"

"I'm waiting for instructions. I don't want to do anything to put your people at risk. But, now, since you've told me who both sides are, I should call that in."

Rodriguez walked away for the fire, took out her satellite phone, and called the control desk, where she reported the new information. The New Islamic Caliphate and Lysenko's group fighting over the mine. This was exactly the sort of situation that she had hoped to avoid by being on the ground here. But the news of the hafnium deposit had moved faster than the village's decision-making. That had always been a risk. Now the fighting could intensify, and the villagers could be permanently displaced or killed. Or other players could find out about the deposit and try to take advantage of the situation. The CIA needed to move fast. She put away her phone and went back to the fire.

"Did they tell you anything?" Anna asked.

Rodriguez shook her head. Then she smiled and tried to put the best spin on it. "They'll know what to do. And they'll be in touch when they have a plan in place."

IN THE MEANTIME, Commander Bashir and his people were back at the camp in the mountain valley that they had set up before they went to Agua Dulce. Ten of his fighters were dead and eight were wounded. He sat on a camp stool near a small fire, talking with Saad.

"Are the wounded being cared for?" Bashir asked.

"We have plenty of medical supplies."

"We'll bury the dead in the morning."

"It's a shame so many died."

"I take responsibility. Someone in the village must have been a spy. I should have expected it."

"They were Lysenko's men," Saad said.

"I know."

"I thought we were allies."

"They are mercenaries. They have no honor. He must have been paid more than we were paying to betray us."

"What will we do now?"

Bashir got out his satellite phone and called the Grand Imam. "I must speak to you."

"Is this an emergency? Why not bring your problem before the council?"

Bashir explained what had happened.

"So you've lost the mine?"

"If we hadn't retreated, we would have all died."

"You're sure it is Lysenko?"

"We saw him during the second battle when he brought rein-forcements."

"He still owes us for the Soviet weapons."

"If he's turned against us, maybe they weren't really confiscated. Maybe he sold them to someone else."

"We heard a rumor that he was working with the Blaze Group now."

"That would explain the mercenary reinforcements."

"What will you do now? We cannot offer any help from here."

"This is my problem. I will take back the mine."

"Go with Allah."

Bashir ended the call.

"What now?" Saad asked.

"Our convoy bringing the rest of the mining equipment should arrive at Agua Dulce the day after tomorrow. How many fighters are with them?"

"Ten."

Bashir took out a tablet computer where he'd saved a map of the area. "Choose two men, send them around the village to meet our convoy on the main road and guide them to this area." He pointed to a valley east of Agua Dulce. "It's close enough to strike at the temple, but far enough away not to be seen."

"We won't be able to hide from the locals."

"The locals don't matter."

He wrote a note and handed it to Saad. "The convoy must stay hidden until we're ready to move against the mercenaries."

"Yes, Commander."

Saad walked off into the dark.

Bashir pushed a log into the fire with his boot. The council would judge him harshly for this setback. If he couldn't retake the mine, his girls might be young women before he could find a way to get back to Iraq. And he would never become a member of the council with such a blot on his record. Lysenko only worked for money. Why had the Blaze Group hired him? And why did that mean that he had to betray the Caliphate? Well, they would find out soon enough. And after Lysenko told him what he wanted to know, he would have him killed, and the Blaze Group would discover the true wrath of jihad.

11

The next morning, at the NDA building in Suitland, Maryland, KD and Blunt sat in Garcia's office. A series of detailed satellite images were displayed on a flatscreen TV hanging on the wall.

"Two factions are fighting over the mine at Agua Dulce," Garcia said. "Satellite surveillance two days ago captured a picture of Abu Bashir at a fortified position surrounding the temple. He's on the priority watch list. He's with a jihadist group, the New Islamic Caliphate. They used to control the mine. The Lysenko Group pushed them out and took over yesterday."

"So Lysenko has been after the ore all along," KD said.

Garcia continued. "Because the State Department is negotiating with the Chileans and Bolivians, State doesn't want a large CIA presence down there. That's where you come in. The CIA geologist—Cora Rodriguez—is still down there. She has some locals with her. You two are going to drop in, help her and the locals keep these factions off balance until State can work something out and send in the cavalry."

KD glanced at Blunt and then looked back at Garcia. "What're our parameters?"

"Don't kill any locals or destroy their property. Otherwise, improvise. Play nice with the CIA operator. Tina will provide all the background you need. You leave out of Joint Base Andrews in three hours."

KD hurried across town to her apartment. She changed out of her civilian dress clothes and put on desert camouflage. After she tied her boots, she took her backup Glock from the shelf in the bedroom closet and put it in the duffel with her spare clothes and shower kit. She'd get the rest of her tactical gear from the weapons locker at NDA headquarters.

As she turned from her side of the closet, she saw Frank's crumpled boxer shorts lying on the carpet on his side of the bed. She smiled. His tidiness hadn't improved since their divorce. She opened his side of the closet. Dress shirts, ties, two suits—the clothes he needed when he was in town. She held his black suit coat up to her face and breathed in his scent. Maybe she was being too hard on him. Maybe she should just let him move in. She let go of his suit and shut the closet doors. Not now. Now wasn't the time to make any important decision. She needed her mind clear. All that mattered was the mission. Her and Blunt and the mission.

She got out her personal phone and texted Frank. "I'm on the road. Love you." Then she turned off her phone, set it down on her night table, and plugged in its charging cord.

Fifteen hours later, KD and Blunt sat on the fold-down seats in the back end of a small plane flying low through the foothills of the Andes mountains in the dark, bouncing along with the wind gusts. Blunt gripped the sides of his seat with both hands. "Jesus, glad I'm wearing a helmet. The last bump could have knocked me out."

KD smiled. "You pack your chute?"

"Don't trust anyone else. You should have let me pack yours."

"I think I'll take my chances. You read up about Rodriguez?"

"Yep."

"How do you feel about her?"

"She looks like a solid operator. A little iffy, maybe, on her combat training, but that's not her game."

"Yeah, but anyone who can work by themselves in a situation as tight as the one she's in has got to have skills."

"That's for sure."

The pilot spoke over the comms. "We're six minutes out."

Blunt slid open the side door behind the wing while KD positioned two crates of gear in the doorway.

"I hear they got a problem with dry lightning in these mountains," Blunt said.

"Looks okay thus far." KD sniggered. "I'll let you know if the hair starts standing up on my arms."

The pilot's voice came over the comms. "Now."

They pushed the crates out, and then KD, followed by Blunt, jumped out of the airplane. The ground came up fast. The parachutes opened, and they floated down into a small field near a mountain stream. Working in the moonlight, they rolled up the parachutes and opened the crates to take out their seventy-pound backpacks. Then they flattened the crates and buried the parachutes, helmets, and crates. "How far off are we?" Blunt asked.

"Not too far," KD replied. She took a small tablet computer out of her backpack and engaged the GPS. "About half a mile." She pointed with her left hand. "Main road is about two miles to our right, the village is more or less straight ahead of us, and Rodriguez is somewhere left of the village."

"Can we track her sat phone?"

"It's not on." She put the tablet in her pants cargo pocket. "Latest intel has the jihadis in the mountains and Lysenko at the village."

Blunt took his assault rifle out of his pack and screwed on the silencer. KD did the same.

"You ready?"

He nodded.

They pulled on their backpacks and started up the hill, carrying their rifles in front of them two-handed.

Later, at midmorning, while they were crossing a ridge, they spotted a pair of Lysenko's men guarding a dirt road that switch-backed down to a valley. They lay down in the brush. KD pulled out the tablet and looked at a map. "Village must be on the other side of the next ridge," she whispered.

Blunt nodded.

"So we're going to slip between these two and the village, then move up to the high ground across the way to see what's going on in Lysenko's camp."

RODRIGUEZ SAT NEXT to Roberto and Anna at the spent fire. Three more families had found them in the night, bringing their number up to seven families—fourteen adults and eleven children. The timer on her watch went off. She walked off several yards, took out her satellite phone, and input the emergency number and security code.

"Speak."

"Checking in."

"Two NDA operatives are on the ground, working their way toward you."

"What's the mission?"

"Continue to ally yourself with the villagers and disrupt both the Caliphate and Lysenko. As long as they're fighting each other, no mining can take place."

"Roger."

"The NDA operatives will track you via your sat phone, so keep it charged."

She ended the call, took the solar charger out of her go-bag, and plugged in the satellite phone. Then she went back to her place beside Roberto. He looked at her questioningly.

She spoke in English. "I've heard back from my people. Two oper-atives are coming to help us."

"What will they do?"

"We're going to keep the Caliphate and Lysenko's fighters from mining."

"How will that help?"

"We don't want criminals or religious fighters to have the ore. And we don't think you should be coerced. We think the ore should only be mined in a respectful, sustainable way."

Anna put her hand on Roberto's arm. "Tell her."

"I don't know."

"You have to. Tell her or I will."

"What do you need to tell me, Roberto?" Rodriguez asked.

"We're in favor of mining. We do think the village should enter the twenty-first century. But Juan Carlos promised to pay us for information about the village meetings. We're going to use that money to go back to the US to find doctors to help little Roberto. We didn't intend for anyone to get hurt."

"No one can blame you for wanting to help your son. How did you hurt anyone?"

"Tomas's cousin Gomez was working for the Caliphate. He told them where the mine was. Well, now it looks like Juan Carlos was working for Lysenko. I didn't tell Lysenko where the mine was—the Caliphate had already taken it when I called him—and I wouldn't have helped him if I'd known who he was. But if neither side knew where the mine was, we wouldn't have this fighting. Anyway, I'm sorry for my part in this. And I want to do whatever I can to make up for it."

"Do you really mean that?"

"I do."

"Then talk to your neighbors. See if they'll help us work against both the Caliphate and Lysenko."

"I will."

MEANWHILE, Colbert met the airplane carrying Lysenko's reinforcements at the smugglers' airstrip. Twelve men wearing body armor climbed out of the plane carrying their gear and extra ammunition, which they loaded into Colbert's Humvee. Colbert turned to the pilot. "Where are the rocket-propelled grenades?"

"It'll be a couple of days," the pilot said.

"I want them ASAP," Colbert said.

"When I get them, you'll get them."

The pilot got back into the cockpit and took off down the runway. Colbert drove the men up the switchbacks to Agua Dulce, where he deployed them to the outer perimeter.

The villagers who stayed in the village were already going about their daily lives. The helicopter carrying the engineers from Iquique, Chile, arrived just after lunch. The engineers immediately went into the mine and began formulating a plan to extract the ore.

"How soon can mining start?" Lysenko asked.

"As soon as the materials, equipment, and workers get here," the lead engineer replied. "If we make an order today, you'll start construction of the infrastructure in a week to ten days."

"That long?"

"You can't fly the equipment in. That many cargo planes would pancake that makeshift runway. Then you'd have no way to fly in here at all."

"What about the equipment that's already here?"

"It's a start, but not nearly enough. And who's going to do the work? Mining, particularly opening a mine, is skilled work. If you want to do this right and preserve the site, we'll be able to get started in a week to ten days."

KD AND BLUNT lay under cover of heavy brush on a rise to the west of Agua Dulce, where they had an excellent view of the village and the temple through their binoculars. The armored personnel carrier sat directly behind the gate. The fence surrounding the temple compound was reinforced with razor wire, and dirt was piled into berms around the machine gun placements. The Humvees sat in a row in the middle of the compound with the supply trucks. A helicopter was parked at the east end. They watched a Humvee crowded with men roll down the main street, headed for the compound.

"Blunt, isn't that Colbert in the front passenger's seat?"

Blunt adjusted his binoculars. "Good call, Doc. That's definitely him. So this really is Lysenko's crew. Looks like they're getting ready for round two."

"The jihadis came for the ore. They're not going to give up so easily."

"Neither are we."

KD got out her tablet and opened the map. "Rodriguez's sat phone is on. She's just a couple of miles west of here. Time to get moving."

ABOUT AN HOUR LATER, as KD and Blunt were walking down a narrow trail, they spotted Rodriguez and the villagers at the pond by the rock outcropping where they had set up camp. As they approached the group, two of the villagers raised their hunting rifles. KD and Blunt shifted the muzzles of their rifles towards the men.

Rodriguez motioned for everyone to lower their guns. She spoke in Spanish. "Hey, hey, nothing to worry about here," she said.

KD spoke in English. "You Rodriguez?"

"Yes."

"I'm KD and this is Blunt."

Rodriguez turned to the two villagers and spoke in Spanish. "Lower your weapons."

Roberto added, "We're all friends here."

They lowered their guns. KD and Blunt pointed theirs at the ground.

Roberto spoke in English. "Do you want water? We have good water here."

Blunt nodded. "Appreciate it."

Roberto passed him a canteen. He took a long drink and passed the canteen to KD. She drank and passed the canteen back to Roberto. "Thanks."

KD and Blunt slipped off their packs. "No one's watching your perimeter."

Rodriguez shrugged. "No one is after us. What do you know about what's going on here?"

"Just the general outline."

Rodriguez filled them in.

"So the Caliphate found out where the mine was from Gomez, who's a cousin of one of the elders," KD said.

"Yes," Rodriguez replied.

"And after they took it, Lysenko took it from them."

"Those were his men you saw as you came in."

"And they're holding two relatives of the elder as collateral?"

"That's what the families who showed up yesterday said."

"Where are the jihadis now?"

"They're somewhere northwest of us."

Roberto cut in. "What's your plan?"

"We need more information," KD replied. "If we're going to protect the temple and keep you villagers out of harm's way, we need detailed info about what's happening at the temple."

Roberto, speaking in Quechuan, explained the situation to the villagers. They spoke among themselves for a few minutes. Then Roberto turned to Rodriguez and spoke in English. "Three of us will go to the village and watch. If anything important happens, we'll come back. Otherwise, we'll be back before dark."

Roberto and two others started up the ridge toward Agua Dulce. KD, Blunt, and Rodriguez sat on the ground. "How do you think this will work?" Rodriguez asked.

"It's your party," Blunt replied. "You know the ground. What do you think?"

"There're too many of them between the Caliphate and Lysenko's forces for us to be effective against all of them, even using guerrilla tactics. But while they're fighting, if we can pick off fighters on both sides to keep one side from gaining the upper hand, maybe we can delay them long enough for the State Department to come up with a permanent solution."

"That sounds doable," KD said. She took out her tablet and opened the local map. Rodriguez and Blunt shifted around beside her to look at it.

"What's going on here?" Blunt pointed at a rocky area to the west of the temple.

"There're a series of steep rocks protecting that side. You'd need climbing gear to go up or down from the temple," Rodriguez said.

"And over here?"

"Cliff to the north. Drops about one hundred feet."

"So the only easy way up is via the south or east?"

"Yes. And the only path comes up from the cross street in the village."

KD cut in. "Is there a way to get up on the top of the rocks overlooking the temple? Coming in from the west, maybe?"

"There're animal trails and footpaths meandering all over these hills. We'd have to ask Roberto."

"Up in the rocks, shooting down on Lysenko's men or the jihadis from cover, that would be choice," Blunt said.

Juan Carlos, wearing a light backpack, stood on a ridge looking down at the villager's camp by the pond. This was the third place he'd come to. He hadn't thought they would be hiding so close to Agua Dulce, but it showed how little Lysenko, or the jihadis for that matter, knew about the surrounding land. He watched Roberto and two other villagers start up the trail toward the village and cut down a path to intersect with them out of sight of the camp. When they came over a steep hill, he was waiting for them.

"Roberto," he said, speaking in Spanish.

"What are you doing here?"

"Looking for you."

"I've got nothing to say to you. You were Lysenko's puppet all along, and now we've been run out of our village and the temple has been desecrated."

"I was tricked as much as you. My livelihood depends on the goodwill of the villagers all over this country. How do you think I will be treated if what I did gets out?"

"Serves you right."

"Listen. Lysenko contacted me. He asked me to find the villagers who left and convince them to come back."

"Do you think anyone will listen to you?"

"I'm not going to help him. The only reason I'm here is to tell you his plan."

"Well, you've told me."

"I have. Good luck, Roberto." Juan Carlos took off up the trail he'd just come down. He'd done what he could. Now he was going to get far away from here until the fighting was over for certain.

TWO SCOUTS CAME into the jihadi encampment and found Commander Bashir in his tent talking with Saad. "Well?"

"A few men arrived by helicopter. They went into the mine. A number of other men arrived by plane—about twelve or fourteen. More soldiers, I think."

"And the temple?"

"They're dug in, and they've reinforced the fence."

"Thank you. Go back out just before dark."

The scouts left.

"They're in the same situation we were in," Saad said.

"I agree. They're waiting for their equipment and miners."

"It's going to be hard to push them out of there."

"He's already added a dozen men. How many more will he add if we give him time? We have to coordinate with the convoy and attack as soon as possible." Bashir sipped his coffee. "And we have to kill them all, especially Lysenko. I want him out of the way, and I want any other competitors to know what the stakes are."

"I'll radio the convoy and find out when they will be in position." Saad left the tent.

Commander Bashir studied the map of the area. His remaining men would attack from the west, and the fighters from the convoy would attack from the east. Saad was right. They might not have enough men to win, especially attacking a fixed position. They had several rocket-propelled grenades with the convoy. They would certainly make short work of the defenses at the temple, but the risk of caving in the mine and delaying excavation was too high to use them as anything but a last resort. He looked off toward the opening in the tent. What if, instead of outgunning Lysenko, they outmaneuvered him?

He got on his computer, plugged in his satellite phone, and typed an encrypted email to the caliphate council explaining his situation and asking them to negotiate with the Blaze Group to cut off aid to Lysenko. He pressed send and closed his laptop. It was probably a long shot, but anything was worth a try.

ROBERTO and the two other villagers got back to the pond a little after dark. "I am glad to see you made it back," Rodriguez said in Quechuan.

"What did you see?" KD asked.

Roberto spoke in English. "Everything is calm in the village. Lysenko's people are busy at the temple, organizing their supplies and improving their defenses."

"So nothing new," Blunt said.

"While we were leaving, we saw two Muslims sneaking up toward the village."

"You sure they were Muslims?"

"Absolutely."

Rodriguez turned to KD. "What do you think? Scouts or saboteurs?"

"Either way," KD said, "the jihadis are advancing their plan. We need to be ready. Roberto, do any of the villagers have military training?"

"No. But we know all the paths and trails. We could show you the best ways in and out of wherever you want to go."

"Is there a trail leading up to the top of the rocks to the west of the temple?"

Roberto nodded. "It's not easy, but yes, there's a trail up the back side."

"We'll need you to show us."

"Of course."

"And we need villagers to be close enough to the village to hear when the jihadis attack and report back to us."

"When do you think it will happen?"

"Soon. As soon as they think they can win."

12

The next morning, just before sunrise, the Caliphate fighters moved in from east and west of Agua Dulce. Lysenko's outer perimeter cameras spotted the vanguard, and his men started skirmishing with the jihadis, backing toward the village, but fighting more forcefully as they began to group together. The mercenaries in the temple compound scrambled out of their cots and took position in the trenches along the fence, their rifles at the ready. Colbert and Lysenko walked the perimeter, making sure that their men were in place and had plenty of ammunition.

When they heard the gunfire, KD and Blunt put on their body armor. Blunt handed Rodriguez his assault rifle and took the sniper rifle from his backpack and assembled it. Then he checked his pistol. He looked up at KD and nodded. "Ready, Doc?"

The villagers hid in a shallow cave in the rocks on the other side of the pond. Anna hugged Roberto tight. "Be safe."

"I will."

Roberto led KD, Blunt, and Rodriguez along the switchback trails up around to the west side of the temple where they set up in a rocky vee in the steep rocks overlooking the temple compound. There were only two guards on this side of the compound because the steep terrain made attacking from this side almost impossible. They settled in, KD and Blunt watching the compound, Rodriguez and Roberto watching their path back down.

As the Caliphate fighters began to gather at the base of the hill and fire up into the temple compound, the mercenaries returned fire. Blunt chose a target with his sniper rifle, the man operating the fifty-caliber machine gun at the southeast corner, who was firing downhill toward the village. Blunt pulled the trigger. The man fell sideways. Another man pulled him out of the way and a third man took his place.

KD lowered his binoculars and tapped Blunt on the shoulder. At the base of the hill, a jihadi was using a villager as a shield, crouching behind the man with his hand on the man's left shoulder and his rifle barrel resting on the man's right shoulder. They zigzagged up the slope, bullets striking around them, no one wanting to shoot the villager. Blunt got the pair in his scope and waited. Every few steps, the jihadi peeked around the left side of the villager. Blunt aimed for that spot. When the jihadi's head appeared, Blunt fired. The jihadi fell, and the villager dove for cover.

Then Lysenko's mercenaries opened the gate and the armored personnel carrier started slowly down the hill, its machine gun scattering the jihadis.

"They're screwed now," Blunt said.

A jihadi ran out from the woods into the middle of the path, put a rocket propelled grenade launcher to his shoulder and fired. The machine gun on the armored personnel carrier exploded. The armored personnel carrier started backing up the hill. Another jihadi ran out onto the path with another grenade launcher but was shot down before he could fire it. A third jihadi ran out, picked up the launcher and fired, blowing out the front left wheel on the armored personnel carrier. Three men climbed out of the carrier and ran up the hill under cover fire.

"Didn't expect that," KD said.

"So much for the armored personnel carrier," Blunt said.

"Going to have to take out a few more of Lysenko's people to keep both sides balanced," KD said.

So it went for almost three hours, KD spotting and Blunt firing to keep the jihadis from making it all the way up to the compound and to balance out the dead and injured, taking their time, being careful to not be spotted, until a round chipped the boulder to the right of Blunt's head.

"Incoming," KD said.

Blunt ducked. KD swung around with her binoculars. Another bullet flew by a few inches above Blunt. "Jihadi with a high-powered rifle, about halfway down the slope to the left of the path."

Blunt sprang up and scanned the slope for the man through his rifle scope. He spotted him crouched behind a tree. "He's got excellent cover."

The jihadi's head popped out. Blunt fired. The round hit the tree. "Can't get him from here."

Blunt squatted and looked over the rocks around them for a better spot to shoot from. Another bullet zipped by over their heads. "We're going to have to wait him out."

They sat in the rocks, waiting, an occasional round flying by over their heads until KD worked around to a two-inch crack between two boulders where she could look through one lens of her binoculars. "Nothing has changed. Jihadis are stalled on the hill. Wait a minute. I think our guy is gone."

She moved back to her old spot and peered down at the tree. No one. She scanned the area. He was gone.

Blunt popped up and looked down through his rifle scope. "Jihadis are retreating, I think."

"Let's get out of here before they cut off our way back to the pond."

KD, Blunt, Rodriguez, and Roberto made their way down the ridge following the foot paths, keeping well away from the jihadists moving toward their camp to the northwest. When they reached the pond, they found the other villagers hidden in the cave where they'd left them. Anna rushed out carrying her daughter in one arm and holding her son's hand with her other hand.

She hugged them all to Roberto. "I'm so glad you're safe."

"What happened?" one of the other villagers asked.

Roberto explained, speaking in Quechuan.

KD, Blunt, and Rodriguez stood together away from the others. "What's our plan for tomorrow?" Rodriguez asked. "Do we stick with this plan or try something new?"

"I think this plan is working," KD said. "Both sides are weaker, and no one is winning."

Blunt nodded. "But that doesn't mean we can't whittle down the jihadis. As long as they don't leave, Lysenko can't mine. But they don't have to be winning."

BASHIR LED his combined forces back to their encampment in the mountain valley west of Agua Dulce, carrying their wounded and dead. They'd managed to inflict casualties on Lysenko's mercenaries, but they hadn't been able to make any real progress. Another day like this and they'd have to pull back.

"Saad, see to the wounded and give me a count of the dead. And form a burial detail. We'll attend to them tonight."

"Yes, Commander."

Bashir went into his tent and sat down with his laptop. What could he do? The miners and mining equipment were still in the valley to the east of Agua Dolce. But they wouldn't be much use taking the mine back. What they were short on was fighters. He went online and clicked on his encrypted email. A reply from the Caliphate Council. He opened it. They'd reached an accord with the Blaze Group. They would cut off aid to Lysenko and send mercenaries to aid Bashir's fighters just in case Lysenko wouldn't surrender. The Caliphate would start mining and then hand the mine over to the Blaze Group later. Blaze would refine the ore and share the hafnium with the Caliphate. Blaze needed Lysenko's weapons connection, so he had to be kept alive.

Bashir smiled. Letting Lysenko live was a small price to pay for such a big win. He typed, "When will the mercenaries arrive?"

The reply was almost immediate. "They'll arrive at the airstrip in the morning."

He closed his laptop. Tomorrow they'd be back at the temple compound.

Saad came into the tent. Bashir looked up. "Well?"

"Everything is prepared for the burials. We lost ten men. Two are badly wounded. Five have minor wounds."

"Not too bad, but bad enough."

"What are our plans?"

"The Blaze Group has switched sides."

"Allah be praised."

"They're sending mercenaries to help us. They arrive tomorrow."

"Are you sure it's not a trap?"

"It was negotiated by the Council, so I'm sure precautions were taken."

"Tomorrow then."

"Yes, tomorrow. There is much to do once we control the mine."

MEANWHILE, at the Temple encampment, Colbert was walking along the perimeter directing their people to improve their defenses.

"Set the fifty-caliber gun over about a foot to the right," Colbert said. "We'll cover more of the open ground to the left of the armored personnel carrier wreckage."

Two men started moving the machine gun tripod.

"That's better."

Lysenko came over. "How many men have we lost?"

"Fourteen down between dead and wounded. If they attack again, we need reinforcements."

Lysenko went to his tent for his satellite phone and called his contact at the Blaze Group.

"Lysenko, I was just about to call you."

"I need more men, ASAP."

"That's not possible."

"Why not?"

"We've made a deal with the Caliphate. The mine is theirs now. You can wave a white flag and retreat."

"Where do I fit into this deal?"

"You don't. You're out. I'm sorry, but the Caliphate believes you double-crossed them, and they won't work with a double-crosser."

"But this is all your doing. You sent me here. And now you're telling me I'm out on this deal, and I've lost the Caliphate as a customer?"

"There's nothing we can do about it. The reinforcements for the Caliphate will arrive in the morning. Get out of there while you can." He ended the call.

Lysenko set down his phone. Christ. Who else could he call? No one who could get here by tomorrow. Or even the next day, for that matter. He stepped out of his tent and looked at the temple. This ore was the future. He had to have a piece of the action, and if the Caliphate and Blaze wouldn't cut him in, he was going to have to cut them out. It was a gamble. The odds were long, but it was worth the chance. They had the high ground, and they were dug in. All his people were professional soldiers. They'd signed on knowing the risk. And if they won, he'd be mining without partners. He'd have to get reinforcements from another cartel, but that was Blaze's fault, not his.

He found Colbert directing men who were repairing holes in the southeast chain-link fence. "Got a minute?"

They walked away from the work detail. "What's up?"

"Blaze won't send any help."

"Why not?"

"They made a deal with the Caliphate."

"Then we should get out of here."

"I'm going to fight."

"Are you crazy? We might last through tomorrow, but then what will we do the next day? There is no upside."

"Give me one more day. The Caliphate must be out of resources if they're willing to partner with Blaze. We fight them off tomorrow, they might fold. I think it's worth the chance. One more day. You'll get your bonus either way."

"Are you going to tell the men?"

"No. Some of them might run."

Colbert looked around the compound. "So this is all the men we're going to have?"

"Yes. It's going to be a close thing, but we're going to win. I can feel it."

"Okay. I'll give you one more day, but if the tide turns, I'm out of here."

BACK AT THE villager camp by the pond, KD, Blunt, and Rodriguez were guarding the perimeter while the villagers prepared food. KD's satellite phone buzzed.

"Thorne speaking."

"KD? Garcia here. We've intercepted some intel. Blaze and the New Islamic Caliphate have reached an agreement to share the ore. Lysenko is out."

"So the jihadis are going to get the mine?"

"Yes."

"And is Lysenko walking away, or are his fighters joining forces with the jihadis and Blaze?"

"We don't know. You need to keep the fighting going as long as possible. An NDA strike team is being assembled, but they won't be there until tomorrow evening."

"I thought we couldn't have much of a footprint here."

"State changed its mind. Nobody mines the hafnium."

"The jihadis will be in control of the mine tomorrow. After that, even with the strike team's help, we won't have enough personnel to take the mine."

"Those are your orders. Keep fighting. No one mines."

"Tell the strike team to bring a reconnaissance drone," KD said. "And one of those new mini-cluster-bomb drones."

"I'll see what I can do."

"We've got to have the bomb drone if we're going to stand a chance."

KD ended the call and motioned to Blunt and Rodriguez. After they came over, she told them about her conversation with Garcia.

"So how does this change our plans?" Rodriguez asked.

"We need villagers scouting the temple. Is Lysenko staying or leaving? How many of his fighters are there? How many jihadis are going to be there?"

"We don't have to take the mine to keep them from mining," Rodriguez said.

"No, we don't."

"We don't have the people to defend the temple encampment anyway," Blunt added.

"Strike team will be here tomorrow evening. Until then we need to be particularly careful."

KD called Roberto over and explained the situation.

"What do you need from us?" Roberto asked.

"First, we need two of you surveilling the temple encampment. If Lysenko's people leave, we need to know."

"Okay, I'll get one of the others to go with me."

"No, we need you to go into the village and organize your people to evacuate. If we start fighting tomorrow, we don't want them to be caught in the crossfire."

"We don't have to run. We can fight."

"Then organize your people to fight. You have a satellite phone?"

"Yes. Juan Carlos lent me one."

KD wrote her satellite phone number on a scrap of paper and handed it to him. "You go into town. Organize the evacuation and resistance. Evacuate to this location. Fighters should gather on this side of the first ridge west of town. Stay out of the way of the jihadis until they're on the path from the village to the temple. We want them all together so that we can cut at their flanks and catch them in the crossfire."

Roberto talked with the villagers. Two men took off on the trail toward the temple encampment. Roberto hugged Anna and then came back to KD, Blunt, and Rodriguez. "I'm off to the village."

"Call us when you've got your people organized."

IT WAS dark by the time Roberto came over the last ridge and made his way down into the village. The villagers were gathered at the plaza in front of the church, torches lighting the space. The church and the nearby buildings were pockmarked with bullet holes. There were three fresh graves in the small graveyard beside the church. Roberto spotted Tomas and Maria and went to them.

"Tomas, Maria, I glad you're still safe."

"So much trouble," Tomas replied. "I never thought I would call the ore a curse."

"No one could have known what would happen," Roberto replied.

"Where is your family?" Maria asked.

"You know the little pond down to the west? The one with the cave?"

She nodded.

"There. There're other families there too, and Cora Rodriguez and two other Americans."

Gomez approached them. "Why are you here?"

"There will be more fighting tomorrow. I've come to help those who want to evacuate."

"The Muslims promised no one would get hurt."

"And we have three new graves. Whose are they?"

"The Paucars' children," Tomas said.

"All three of their children murdered? So much for Muslim promises," Roberto said. "You should hang your head in shame, Gomez."

"I am ashamed."

"You should give the money they paid you to help rebuild the village."

"I will."

"Are you just saying that? Or do you mean it?"

"I mean it."

"So you're ready now to put our people first?"

"Yes."

"Somehow I don't believe you."

"Enough arguing," Tomas said. He put his hand on Roberto's shoulder and shouted, "Gather around! Gather around!"

The villagers gathered in a tight circle around them. Then Tomas turned to Roberto. "Talk to the people."

"The Caliphate and Lysenko's fighters fought to a draw today, but they may be on the same side tomorrow. At first light, the Caliphate will probably go to the temple. Senora Rodriguez and two more Americans are making a plan to protect our temple and sacred ore. A few of your neighbors and I are helping them. If you want to join us, get your hunting rifle and come with me. Everyone else should gather supplies for a few days and go to the pond by the cave in the valley to the west if they want to stay out of the fighting. Some of our people are already there."

"Why should we trust the Americans?" Gomez asked.

"Because they have helped us when the others have not. We don't have to trust them in everything, just in protecting the ore for now."

Tomas cut in. "I will stand with you, Roberto. We've had our differences, but in this you are right. Neighbors, go to the pond or come with us, but make your decision before dawn."

Roberto got out his satellite phone and called KD. "Expect a number of villagers to arrive at the pond before dawn. I'm guessing maybe seven men will be with me on the other side of the ridge."

"Wonderful. Remember, don't engage with the jihadis. Let them pass. Wait until you hear from me so we can coordinate our strategy."

GOMEZ WENT BACK to his one-room house and got his satellite phone out of the cutout behind the kerosene stove. Roberto was right. He was only in it for the money and his own future. The Paucars should have taken better care with their children, and they wouldn't have been caught in a crossfire. Bashir and his people were on the run. If only he'd paid him when he promised, he could have left before the fighting. But now, Bashir retaking the temple was his only chance to get paid. The villagers had chosen poorly. If they got involved in the fight, they'd be slaughtered like the Paucars. But that's what they got for siding with the Americans. He'd earned his fee. He deserved it. He had to do whatever he could to get at least part of it. He called Bashir.

"Commander?"

"Speaking."

"The Americans are organizing the people to fight against you and Lysenko."

He snorted. "The villagers? Against both of us? What can they do?"

"I'm not sure. They're evacuating the village."

"That's a smart move if they think there's going to be more fighting."

"And some of the men are gathering under Roberto and Rodriguez's leadership."

"If you can stop them from doing anything foolish, you should. We don't want to hurt them, but we will kill them if they fight against us."

"I'm compromised. They know that I helped you, so they won't listen to me any longer."

"So be it."

"But our deal is still on?"

"You're still expecting payment after all that has happened?"

"We made a deal."

"You're right, but right now we're short on cash. Fighting is expensive. When we're in control of the mine, I'll see what I can do." Bashir ended the call.

Gomez laid his phone down on the table. Bashir was lying. He wasn't going to pay him now that he didn't have to. He should have gotten the money before he told them where the mine was. He'd thought he had a relationship with the Muslims, a relationship built on trust, but now he knew they thought of him as just another infidel.

When the fighting was done, no matter which group won, he

would not be accepted in the village. So he had to hang on, just in case he could be useful to Bashir and extract some sort of payment, any amount of money that would help him start over. Tonight he was safe in his house. But tomorrow? He couldn't stay in the village. It was too dangerous. And if he went to the pond, he might end up as collateral damage. Where could he hide until the fighting was over?

13

Shortly before dawn, villagers began to trickle in at the camp at the pond. Anna stood by the trail, hugging the women and pointing out open areas where the newcomers could set up camp. While they were settling in, the two men who'd been surveilling the temple compound came into camp and spoke to Rodriguez.

Rodriguez found KD and Blunt. "Lysenko's people are dug in."

"So we're going to be fighting Lysenko's fighters and the jihadis," Blunt said.

"Rodriguez," KD said, "I want you to go with Roberto and the villagers. They know you, and you've got combat experience. Use hit and run tactics. Don't get surrounded, or you'll be massacred."

"Don't worry about us," she said.

"While you all are harassing the jihadis on their way up to the temple, Blunt and I will be picking them off from the high point we used yesterday, so we can evaluate what Lysenko's doing."

"You keep my assault rifle," Blunt said. He dug into his backpack and came out with five extra magazines. "Here's the ammunition. Make it last until you can take more off the jihadis."

"Thanks," Rodriguez said.

Rodriguez, KD, and Blunt shook hands. "Good luck," KD said.

MEANWHILE, a contingent of jihadis were at the smugglers' airstrip as a plane landed with Blaze Group mercenaries. When their captain got off the plane, Saad strode over to him. "Welcome, Captain Adamski. Commander Bashir is waiting up at Agua Dulce."

"I've got twenty men. Have you got enough transport to make it in one trip?"

"We'll manage, Captain."

They rolled up the mountain switchbacks, the sun rising over the mountains to the east. Commander Bashir was waiting for them by Rodriguez's cabin.

"Glad to see you, Captain," Commander Bashir said.

"What's the situation?"

"Lysenko is dug in at the temple compound. We cannot, I repeat, cannot damage the temple. The mine entrance is inside."

"How many men?"

"We think we were evenly matched before you arrived."

Adamski took out his binoculars and looked across to the temple. "So we have to breach the perimeter. Looks like there're only a few ways up. We'll need to move fast if we want to avoid casualties." He put his binoculars down. "Let's get this done."

Adamski divided his men into three fire teams and sent them up three side trails to the top of the hill, while Bashir focused his fighters on the main path.

RODRIGUEZ, Roberto, and the village fighters were hiding in a gulley to the west of Agua Dulce when they saw the jihadi/Blaze fighters starting up the hill toward the temple. Rodriguez called KD on the satellite phone. "You're not going to believe this, but the Caliphate has Blaze reinforcements and they're moving up the hill to the temple like they're going to attack."

"Are you serious?"

"Several teams are moving up the narrow trails from the south and the jihadis are massing at the bottom of the main path."

"Let's hope they obliterate each other. I'll be back in touch after we get into position."

AT THE TEMPLE COMPOUND, Colbert was walking along the perimeter, making sure both machine gun placements were well stocked with ammunition. "Here they come," he said. "Wait until they're well within range. We have the tactical advantage. Don't screw it up."

They waited as the jihadis and Blaze mercenaries worked their way up the hill, moving slowly through the woods, finding cover behind boulders and fallen trees until, finally, Colbert yelled, "Choose your targets."

Gunfire erupted from the compound. Six jihadis fell immediately, but the return fire swarmed into the compound.

KD GOT on her satellite phone to Rodriguez. "You were right. Lysenko is fighting the jihadi/Blaze forces. He must be some kind of crazy. Fire at will."

"Roger."

She put away her phone and nodded to Blunt, who set his sniper rifle on a rock ledge farther to the right of where he'd been yesterday, so that he was out of the line of fire he'd been in before. He was still hidden from the temple encampment but had a clear view down the hill on the main path. He started picking off jihadis. KD was several yards uphill from him where she could see into the encampment.

FIGHTING WAS FIERCE ALL MORNING, with Rodriguez and the villagers ambushing jihadis on their west flank, Blunt shooting them from his perch, and KD coordinating their efforts, but Lysenko's people were still being eliminated one by one until they could no longer effectively defend their entire perimeter. That's when a Blaze Group fire team breached the fence between the machine gun placements and charged into the compound.

Colbert crouched behind a supply truck tire, bullets slamming into the truck, shattering the windows and blowing out the tires. Lysenko spotted him and crawled across the open ground from the shipping crates he'd been using for cover. Colbert shook his head. "I told you it was futile."

"Direct the machine gunners to fire on the enemy in the compound."

Colbert glanced around the side of the tire. A group of jihadis stormed the gate, took out the machine gun, and joined the fire team. "You're on your own." He rushed toward the nearest tent, bullets buzzing around him, and dived through the door flap. Then he crawled to the back, cut a hole through the fabric with his lock-back knife, and stuck his head out to check for enemies. No one. He rolled out onto the dirt and ran at a crouch for the back fence, where he'd cut the chain link the night before. He wriggled through the opening and started climbing down the one-hundred-foot cliff, finding hand and feet holds in the rock. About halfway down he heard thunder and caught a glimpse of lightning from the corner of his eye just before another peal of thunder. He picked up his pace.

Back in the compound, Lysenko kept firing from the cover of the truck. His men were all dying around him as the jihadis and Blaze fire teams overran the compound. As he ejected the empty magazine from his pistol and pushed in his last one, Saad and three others rushed the truck.

"Take him alive," Saad yelled.

The first man tackled Lysenko, grabbing his gun hand. Lysenko fired wide. Then the other two were on him, pinning him to the ground.

"Enough," Saad said. "If we wanted to kill you, you'd already be dead."

Lysenko lay still.

"Handcuff him and keep him under guard."

. . .

KD CALLED RODRIGUEZ. "The temple compound has been overrun. Disengage and head back to the pond. We're going to reconnoiter the situation."

"Will do," Rodriguez replied.

KD and Blunt made their way down the steep hillside, sticking to the cover provided by the jagged rocks. When they reached the trees, they started south at a jog. KD's satellite phone beeped. She looked at the screen. "The strike team is on the ground."

They moved along the ridge, keeping an eye out for jihadis or escaped Lysenko mercenaries. "There's two," Blunt whispered, pointing in the distance to two Middle Eastern men going through the pockets of some dead mercenaries.

"There were—what—fifteen up at the compound?"

"And a few more still climbing the slope."

"So about twenty so far."

They moved around the west side of the village. Two three-man teams of jihadis were going through the clay brick houses, looking for Lysenko's fighters, but they didn't seem to be finding anyone.

"Generous guess," Blunt said, "would be thirty total."

"Lots of dead."

Lightning flashed to the north and the thunder boomed. "That's close," Blunt said.

They climbed a nearby ridge and crawled under some brush. KD got out her binoculars and looked at the temple compound. Some Jihadis and Blaze fighters were dragging the dead to a truck and piling them in the bed, while others were repairing the perimeter fence. "They're cleaning up."

"Drone," Blunt said.

KD put down her binoculars and looked at the sky above the compound. A drone was flying in a slow circle. "That's one of the new ones, isn't it?"

"Looks like it."

A Blaze mercenary pointed up. Another one started shooting at the drone, but it flew away. A few minutes later the truck loaded with the dead came down the path to the village. Lightning flashed to the east. Thunder echoed through the mountains. "A little farther away," Blunt said.

"Let's get back to the pond," KD said.

MEANWHILE, Colbert made his way east of the temple compound, avoiding any contact with jihadis, the Blaze fire teams, or any remaining Lysenko fighters. As he rounded the east side of the deserted village, he heard sporadic firing to the west and then more thunder. At the top of the ridge past a small cabin, he found a Jeep. He hotwired it. It had two-thirds of a tank of gas. He didn't know how far the gas would take him, but he knew it would get him away from here.

He lay his pistol in his lap and started down the switchbacks. If he could get anywhere where he could use a phone, he'd be able to get himself out of this mess. Lysenko was probably dead by now. Some people couldn't be convinced to do what made sense. Mining the hafnium wasn't the only way to make money. Selling and smuggling weapons was always going to be the biggest slice of the pie. Most factions and autocrats couldn't afford a nuclear program.

He saw two jihadis guarding the last switchback leading down to the gravel road in the valley. When they saw him, they stepped into the road and opened fire. He floored the Jeep and roared straight toward them. They dove out of the way at the last minute. He careened around the corner, swerving back and forth across the road and finally regaining control as he reached the gravel road in the valley. He glanced over his shoulder. No one was after him. His windshield was shattered, and he'd taken a glancing round into his Kevlar vest, but somehow he hadn't been killed. If his luck held up, he'd be back in Europe within the week.

. . .

GOMEZ HAD BEEN HIDING in a rock outcropping to the west of the village, listening to the fighting, but since the gunfire had become sporadic, he'd crept out to see what was going on. The battle seemed to be over, but whenever he saw fighters, he hid until they passed by. He didn't want to answer their questions or risk being shot or robbed.

As he came over a ridge to the west of Agua Dulce, he saw three fighters far to his left. He crouched behind a tree. The men were standing together, passing a bottle around. Then, far to his right, he saw the two Americans moving down a trail parallel to his own. He lay down in the path and waited.

KD AND BLUNT stopped at a secluded spot on a hunting trail, where KD took out her satellite phone and called the strike team.

"Captain Thorne? Sergeant Ables here."

"What's your position?"

"About two klicks out. We ran a drone out to survey the situation."

"We saw it. So did the enemy. Move to the west of the temple, home in on my signal, we'll rendezvous with the villagers."

"Roger that."

At a fork in the trail, Blunt heard indistinct talking in the distance. He raised his hand to signal silence. They crept down the trail about thirty yards. Around the next turn, they saw three mercenaries in the distance. They crept closer.

"Who goes first?" one of them asked.

"Rocks, paper, scissors?"

The third mercenary nodded.

The men faced each other, standing over a person on the ground, and played the game. KD and Blunt lay down on the trail. KD trained her silenced assault rifle on the man to the left and fired twice. The first bullet caught him in the shoulder outside his Kevlar vest and spun him sideways. The second hit him in the neck. As he fell, the other two mercenaries pulled their pistols. The man on the right got off a shot before Blunt shot him first in the leg and then in the head. The remaining man turned to run. KD fired a burst that caught both his thighs.

Then KD and Blunt sprang up and ran to the fallen mercenaries. A village girl, maybe twelve, was lying on the dirt with her hands tied behind her.

Blood ran from the mercenary's legs. "Please," he said. "Let me go. I'll crawl out of here."

KD and Blunt exchanged a glance. Blunt pulled his survival knife and cut the man's throat.

KD cut the girl's hands free and then rolled her over. She had a black eye and her face was dirty and scratched. KD put two fingers to her neck. "She's breathing."

Blunt glanced around in a circle. "Too much noise. We need to get out of here." He lifted the girl over his shoulder, and they started down the trail, KD in front.

Gomez watched as the Americans picked up the girl and took off. They hadn't searched the dead men or taken their gear. He waited until they were out of sight before he made his way down the hill to where the men lay. Three assault rifles, two pistols, and two knives that he could see. He didn't want to take a rifle. Someone might think he was a fighter and shoot him. Besides, he didn't have any experience using such a weapon. He picked up the Glock pistol, checked the magazine, and tucked it into his belt. Then he noticed a pair of binoculars. He took them as well. Then he kept on the trail to the pond.

By the time KD and Blunt got back to the pond with the girl, Rodriguez and the village volunteers were already there with the rest of the villagers.

"Rodriguez, Roberto," KD said, "we found this girl along the way."

Blunt laid her gently on the ground.

"This is Claudio's daughter," Anna said. "She went missing last night. What happened to her?"

KD shook her head. "Three mercenaries had her. She was tied up and unconscious."

"I'll find her parents."

Thunder boomed. Roberto looked up the ridge toward the temple. "The lightning storm looks like a bad one. Probably go all night."

"Our strike team got here before the storm."

"Where are they?" Rodriguez asked.

"On the trail. They should be here within a few hours," KD replied.

"What then?" Roberto asked.

"We make a plan to disrupt the jihadis and their Blaze allies."

UP AT THE TEMPLE COMPOUND, Commander Bashir, Saad, and Captain Adamski were supervising the cleanup in the fading light. Lightning crackled in the mountains surrounding them. "Is there a lightning rod?" Bashir asked.

"No," Saad replied. "Not on the temple."

"We need to remedy that. Is all our mining equipment safe?"

"The miners and mining equipment are still down in the valley. I've spoken to the mining superintendent. They'll be ready to drive up here first thing in the morning."

Adamski watched two of his men loading a dead man into the back of a truck. "The assault was even more brutal than I expected. I lost ten men."

"So you have ten left?" Bashir asked.

He nodded.

"And we have fifteen," Saad said. "So that's a total of twenty-five."

"Couldn't be avoided," Bashir said. "Lysenko wouldn't listen to reason after Blaze switched sides."

"It's over now," Saad said.

"What about that drone?" Adamaski asked.

"Probably the Americans," Bashir said.

"So the fighting isn't over?"

"The Americans and the villagers were an annoyance while we were focused on Lysenko, but they won't stand a chance if they come against us now. They're too weak. There's only three Americans, if they're all still alive. And the US can't send in troops without violating national sovereignty, even if they don't know whose. It would be an international incident. They have to wait out the Bolivia-Chile negotiations."

"What about the villagers?"

"I don't think we need to worry about them. They'll trickle back to their homes when they see the fighting is over. Once they realize that we are going to honor our agreement, everything will go back to normal."

"How long do you need for us to stay?" Adamski asked.

"I'll have new fighters here in a week. Until then, I need your help with security."

"What are we going to do with Lysenko?" Saad asked.

"If it were up to me, he'd be dead, but Blaze wants him. They need his black-market connections," Bashir said.

"Do you think he'll cooperate?"

"What choice does he have?"

"Blaze will work to keep Chile and Bolivia from reaching an accord as long as possible," Adamski said.

"That's no more than we expect," Bashir said. "We all want to benefit from the ore as long as we can."

"We should stop work for now. It's been a long day, and the lightning is erratic," Saad said.

"Is the perimeter secure?" Bashir asked.

"Yes," Adamski replied.

"Very well, as soon as they've cleared the dead, the men can stop work until morning."

A FEW HOURS LATER, the seven-person strike team, four men and three women, including a computer tech and a medic, arrived at the camp by the pond, all dressed in body armor and carrying backpacks.

The camp was quiet. Most of the villagers were asleep. KD and Blunt met the strike team at the edge of the camp. "Sergeant Ables?" KD asked.

A man with a gray-stubble crewcut raised his hand. "Right here, ma'am."

"See anything on the trail?"

"We circled wide of the temple. But we did see signs of a few deserters skulking about."

"Your people can settle in on this side of camp," KD said. "You can drop your gear and come with me."

KD, Blunt, and Ables walked down to a cooking fire near the pond, where Rodriguez, Roberto, and Tomas were sitting. Rodriguez stood up. "So your strike team got here."

KD nodded.

"How many?" Roberto asked in Spanish. Rodriguez translated back and forth.

"Seven."

"So that makes ten of you," Tomas said. "And maybe eight villagers who will fight."

"Eighteen total," Roberto said.

"It's enough," KD said.

"What's the plan?" Rodriguez asked.

KD turned to Ables. "Were you able to bring the extra gear I requested?"

"Extra ammunition, hand grenades, a surveillance drone, and a cluster bomb drone. Armorer said the cluster bomb drone was experimental."

"Meaning?"

"He wasn't sure exactly how much damage it would do or how far the spread of the bomblets might be. Better not to be too close when the drone drops it."

She nodded. "We'll use the surveillance drone to watch their movements at the temple compound. Rodriguez and the villagers will create a perimeter at the bottom of the hill to the south and east and fire up at the jihadis if they start down from the compound. Meanwhile, the strike team will take the trail up into the high rocks on the west side where Blunt and I were yesterday. When everyone's in place, we'll use the bomb drone to destroy the machine gun placement farthest to the east, so we don't do any damage to the temple. Then Blunt and I will go in and take out the other machine gun. Meanwhile, the strike team will rappel down into the compound and attack from the west."

"We can do more," Tomas said.

"If your people contain the jihadis until the explosion, they'll be doing plenty. Once we've dealt with the machine guns, you'll be able to work your way up the hill and get into the fight."

"Are you sure the cluster bomb won't damage the temple?" Rodriguez asked.

"A drone has payload restrictions, so it can only carry a limited amount of explosives. The blast should be confined to the machine gun emplacement."

"Which will give us a point of entry," Blunt said.

KD nodded. "With any kind of luck, we'll be able to take out enough jihadi and Blaze fighters so that they won't be able to continue to fight. Then we'll be able to secure the compound." She looked around the group. "Everyone clear as to what they need to do?"

They all nodded.

"Get some sleep. Be ready to go at daybreak."

BASHIR SAT down on his cot and pulled off his boots. His tent was much as he had left it, except for Lysenko's duffel of clothes sitting in the corner. His satellite phone rang. He looked at the screen. It was Gomez. It was a waste of breath talking to him. He let the phone ring and poured water from his canteen into a cup. The phone kept ringing. He drank the water, set down the cup, and then picked up the phone.

"Why are you calling, Gomez? You have nothing to offer."

"Commander, the Americans have received reinforcements."

"Impossible."

"I'm looking at them right now. They parachuted in just before the lightning storm."

"Where are you?"

"Near a pond to the west of Agua Dulce, watching the villagers through my binoculars."

"How many?"

"I count seven soldiers, each carrying large packs."

"So that makes ten Americans total?"

"Yes."

"Keep me informed of their plans."

"I will."

Bashir set down his phone. Ten Americans, and whatever villagers would fight, against their twenty-five seasoned fighters. The villagers were untrained, almost a liability. Plus he was in a fortified position on the high ground. Let them come. It would be a blood-bath. He picked up his walkie-talkie. "Saad?"

"Yes, Commander?"

"Make sure we're ready for battle in the morning."

"You think the Americans will fight?"

"A seven-man team has joined them. I think we should be ready for anything. Call the mining superintendent and have the miners wait in the valley until we contact them tomorrow."

14

At first light, the surveillance drone was flying over the temple compound. The strike team's computer tech sat at a tablet computer, adjusting the flight pattern of the drone and the zoom of the cameras while the tablet recorded the images. KD, Blunt, Rodriguez, and Ables looked at the tablet over her shoulder.

"Nothing's really changed," Blunt said. "Machine guns are in the same places."

"They've repaired the fences," KD said, "and the trenches at the cliff side and the berm at the rocky side are new."

"They're starting to move around," Ables said. "Get the drone out of there before they spot it."

"Okay, Sarge." The technician piloted the drone back behind the first line of trees to the west of the temple. "It's out."

"Good work."

"Get your team moving, Sergeant," KD said.

"Yes, ma'am."

"Good luck," Rodriguez said.

The strike team headed out for the steep trail up the west side of the hill. They wore their body armor and carried their assault rifles at the ready. They'd dumped all the extra gear from their packs and only carried extra magazines of ammunition and their first aid kits.

"Come on, Rodriguez," KD said, "let's find Roberto."

They found Roberto on the far side of the camp near the rocky outcropping eating breakfast with Anna and their children.

"Roberto," KD said, "we need to get moving if we're going to pin them down before any of them go down into the village."

Roberto stood up. "I'll find Tomas and get the people organized."

KD shook Rodriguez's hand. "Keep them out of trouble. Remember, after the explosion they wait until I give the signal to rush the compound."

"We've got our end. See you on the other side."

KD walked back across the camp to where she and Blunt had left their gear. Blunt was checking his rifle. "You ready?"

Blunt nodded. He ran his hands over his vest, touching his spare ammunition magazines, and then patted the sheath of his survival knife.

KD and Blunt made their way along the trails south of Agua Dulce, following the ridge past Rodriguez's cabin. From there they could see the convoy of miners on the main road leading up to Agua Dulce. "We might be in for one hell of a fight if those people get involved," Blunt said.

"Maybe," KD said. "But we've got our orders. If we move quickly enough, we should be able to gain control of the mine until reinforcements arrive."

They continued around the east side of the village until they came to a spot behind a clump of trees that was an easy run to the machine gun placement at the southeast corner of the temple compound. Blunt looked through his binoculars. "Two guys on the machine gun. Another guy close by."

KD took out her satellite phone and called Rodriguez. "You in place?"

"Yes."

She called Ables. "You in place?"

"Affirmative."

"Drop the bomb."

The cluster bomb drone swooped in from the east, dropped its payload, and flew off to the north. KD and Blunt huddled at the base of a tree. The bomblets detonated on impact. When KD looked through her binoculars, the fence was a torn tangle, the machine gun placement was gone, the ground looked as if it had been freshly plowed, and pieces of several men were lying in the dirt. "Let's go," she said.

KD and Blunt rushed up through the knocked down fencing and burning debris, firing as they came, and then charged into the compound, looking for cover on their way to the machine gun placement that faced down the path to the village. Five jihadis opened fire at them from behind a stack of wooden crates near the tents in the center of the compound. They dove behind a truck. "I'll take the right, you take the left," KD said.

Blunt crawled to the front end of the truck. They both fired on the jihadis behind the crates, pinning them down.

Meanwhile, the strike team rappelled down the rocks into the west side of the compound. Three Blaze Group fighters fired on them from behind the berm.

Sergeant Ables swung around on his rappel line and threw a grenade. The Blaze Group fighters scrambled out of the berm, but two took shrapnel. The third retreated backward into the compound, searching for better cover. As the strike team hit the ground, they crossed the berm, finding cover among the supply crates stacked near the north fence. Three of the jihadis behind the stack of crates in the center of the compound shifted position to fire on them.

Meanwhile, KD and Blunt broke cover to rush the machine gun. As Blunt pivoted around the front end of the truck, he got shot three times, twice in his vest and once through his shoulder. He slipped in some muck and fell to the ground behind a dead mercenary. The strike team focused their fire on the jihadis behind the crates at the center of the compound, forcing them down. KD glanced back at Blunt, grimaced, and charged the machine gun placement. The gunner fumbled with his pistol, and KD shot him in the chest before he could pull it clear of his holster. She stood in the machine gun placement and waved her arms at the villagers. The villagers started running up the hill. KD wheeled the machine gun around and fired down the trench that ran along the fence line, killing the jihadi/Blaze fighters before they could scatter.

As soon as the first villagers reached the machine gun, KD ran back to Blunt, who was still lying where he fell. Blood was leaking through the hand he held over the wound in his right shoulder. KD glanced around the compound. "Medic!" she yelled.

The strike team medic slid to his knees on the other side of Blunt, opened his medical kit and tore open the packaging on a quick clot bandage. "I got you covered, buddy."

KD squeezed Blunt's left hand. "Keep it together, Blunt."

"I've been shot worse."

"Looks bad enough."

The medic turned to KD. "I got this."

"Go on," Blunt said.

The villagers were pouring in the gate. KD picked up her rifle and started moving toward the gunfire at the center of the compound.

Meanwhile, Adamski was trying to rally the last few fighters around the entry to the temple, but they were pinned down behind a truck.

"Surrender!" Sergeant Ables called out. "No need for anyone else to die."

Adamski and three fighters—a jihadi and two mercenaries—came out from behind the truck with their hands up.

Ables turned to his men. "Take them into custody."

The strike team took their weapons, searched them, and zip-tied their wrists and their ankles.

KD glanced around the compound. "Where's Bashir?"

"Haven't seen him," Ables replied.

"Leave two men on guard. Have the rest search the compound."

A few minutes later, Ables spotted Bashir and Saad in the distance as they ran through a gap in the tangled fence by the blown-up machine gun placement and started down the slope of the hill. He pointed and yelled. "After them!" Three villagers, running up the hill on the main path, turned and chased them, firing their rifles, but Bashir and Saad disappeared into the trees.

Ables found KD at the center of the compound. "Bashir ran into the woods, but some villagers are after him,"

KD nodded. "That's a tough break. I hope they get him, but we can't spare anyone from here. Our priority is to get this placed buttoned up."

"Yes, ma'am. We'll get on it." He strode off to look for his team.

KD thought through their situation. Fifteen dead jihadis and mercenaries. Three strike team members with nicks and cuts. Four enemy fighters captured. She found Rodriguez, Roberto, and Tomas back near the entrance to the temple. "How many wounded villagers?"

"Only three. Nothing serious," Roberto replied.

"That's great," KD said.

"So the villagers are back in control of the temple," Rodriguez said.

"Maybe," KD said. "There's a convoy of trucks down in the eastern valley. If those are more jihadis or Blaze mercs, we've got more fighting ahead of us."

KD turned to Roberto and Tomas. "Roberto, tell Tomas that you two should go back to the pond camp and bring everyone to the village. We'll set a lookout and work on cleaning up this compound so that we can all fit in here if we need to."

Ables came toward them, pushing Lysenko along in front of him. "Found this one hogtied in a tent."

"Thanks, Sergeant," KD said. She turned to Lysenko. "I'm surprised to find you here."

"You're American," Lysenko said. "Clandestine ops of some kind. Let me go. No one has to know I was here."

Rodriguez cut in. "Let you go? We've been waiting a long time to get our hands on you."

"You can't do anything to me. I haven't broken any laws in the US. You might as well unhook these handcuffs and forget all about me."

"But we're not in the US, or Europe, or anywhere else where we have to follow rules."

"What about Chile or Bolivia?"

"They don't know you're here."

"Ables," KD said, "put the prisoner under guard and don't let him talk to anyone." Ables walked Lysenko back across the compound to where they were keeping the other prisoners.

"That one is a bad man," Roberto said.

Rodriguez nodded. "My government has a lot of questions it wants to ask him."

KD walked across the compound to where Blunt was sitting with his back against the front wheel of a truck. "You're looking better," she said.

"Two in the vest, one in the shoulder. Through and through. Two cracked ribs."

"That must hurt."

"Only if I breathe."

"Upside is you're going home."

"Yep. I'm definitely going to be home for my daughter's dance recital. Wish you were going with me."

"Me, too. But we've still got to finish up here."

"What was the butcher's bill?"

"We were lucky. Three men with minor wounds. Medic took care of them. You, on the other hand, are going out on the medivac."

"You're spoiling me, Doc." Blunt gripped her arm with his left hand.

She patted his hand. "I'll see you when I see you."

KD walked over to the temple where the strike team was guarding the prisoners. "Sergeant, your computer guy have a working sat phone?"

"Yes, ma'am."

"Call in a medivac helicopter."

BASHIR AND SAAD were making their way over the south ridge, heading down the main road to the convoy of miners waiting in the valley when a jeep raced toward them, honking its horn.

Bashir looked over his shoulder. "Gomez."

Gomez screeched to a stop beside them.

"We're glad to see you, brother," Saad said.

"And I'm glad to see you. Villagers with assault rifles are coming this way."

Bashir and Saad climbed into the jeep. "Let's get moving," Bashir said.

"After I'm paid," Gomez replied.

"A mistake. I forgot in all the excitement. I'll take care of that as soon as we're safe."

"Not this time. I drive after I've been paid. Use my sat phone."

"Maybe we kill you and take the jeep," Saad said.

"That would get you away from the fighting, but as soon as you ran into any honest police, you Arabs would be arrested on suspicion of drug trafficking. You need me to get through the roadblocks if you're going to get away from here."

"I'm going to pay, Saad. It's what I agreed to," Bashir said. He turned to Gomez. "Give me the phone."

Gomez handed his satellite phone to Bashir. Bashir glanced back down the road to Agua Dulce. Three villagers were coming toward them in the distance. Bashir input a phone number in the satellite phone and then input a series of account numbers. After he was finished, he handed the phone back to Gomez.

"I've transferred the money."

Gomez called his bank. The money was in his account. He smiled. "Where to?"

"Down to our mining convoy in the valley."

Gomez put the jeep in gear, and they were soon out of range of the villagers. When they reached the convoy of miners and mining equipment waiting in the valley, they found the mining superintendent sitting in a Range Rover at the head of the convoy.

"We've been overrun," Bashir said. "We need your men to fight."

The superintendent shook his head. "Our contract is for mining, not soldiering. But as long as you're paying, we'll wait here until you retake the mine."

Bashir got out his satellite phone, texted the council, and requested more fighters. Four hours later, he got a text in response: *Our resources are depleted. We can't afford to buy more mercenaries, and Blaze won't provide them for free. We need weapons for jihad, and that means we need to concentrate on the drug trade. Go back to Ciudad del Este. Recruit more brothers for the drug routes. Maybe we can revisit the mine business in the future.*

He put away his phone. "They've turned us down. They just don't understand this situation. We could finally control the mine if we had more fighters."

"The council has decided," Saad replied. "We must obey."

"I know," Bashir said. "All the time, all the fighters wasted. We've missed our chance for advancement. Who knows when we'll get to leave this wasteland and go back to Iraq."

"Perhaps it is a sign from Allah that our work here is not finished."

"Perhaps."

Bashir found the mining superintendent. "We're ending your contract."

"Very well," he said. He radioed his truck drivers. They started making U-turns.

Bashir and Saad found Gomez waiting in his jeep under the shade of a small tree. "Where are you going?" Bashir asked.

"To Iquique, Chile. It's a city I know."

"Will you take us?"

"Get in."

"We'll stop along the way and stay with some brothers," Saad said.

"I'm not smuggling on this trip. I don't need to take those kinds of chances anymore."

"Very well," Bashir said. "You're in charge. It's better if you drive."

"To deal with the police, you mean?"

"Of course. We need to get to Iquique without incident."

15

Meanwhile, in Agua Dulce, the villagers had returned to their homes, and KD and the strike team had moved their gear into the tents that were still habitable and were now clearing up the temple compound, gathering the bodies for burial, and repairing the chain-link fence.

Roberto and Tomas came up the hill to inspect the interior of the temple and the mine shaft. KD and Rodriguez went with them. The temple was untouched, and someone had started reinforcing the roof of the mine shaft.

Tomas spoke in Spanish. "We were so lucky."

"How's the village?" Rodriguez asked in English.

"Some stray bullet damage, but that's all. No looting that we know of." Roberto turned to KD. "Sorry about Blunt and your other men."

"Thanks. They'll all be all right."

Roberto turned back to Rodriguez. "How long will these soldiers be staying?"

"Until you've decided who will do the mining and they can take possession," she replied. She switched to Spanish. "Where is the village at with its deliberations?"

"There will be mining, but we haven't decided on the parameters yet," Roberto said.

Tomas nodded. "That's the issue. How will the mining be done? How will our sacred site be kept safe?" He looked at Rodriguez. "Perhaps you would like to make a proposal at the village meeting."

"I'd be honored. When will you meet?"

"Not today. The people are still settling in. But we need to move quickly. We'll call a meeting for tomorrow."

They walked back out of the temple. After Tomas and Roberto said their goodbyes, KD turned to Rodriguez. "What's up?"

Rodriguez filled her in.

"Know what you want to say?"

"I've been waiting for this chance for months."

Ables came over to them. "What do you want to do with the prisoners?"

"That's a good question," Rodriguez said, "but I'm not law enforcement. And we still don't know which country we're in."

KD looked across the compound where the prisoners sat on the ground, handcuffed, the strike team guarding them. "I say we fingerprint them. Anyone with an outstanding warrant gets turned over to the nearest police; everyone else we let go."

"Ship them back to where they came from?" Ables asked.

"We don't want them staying here to cause trouble, so that's probably for the best."

"I agree," Rodriguez said.

"Okay. I'll take care of it," Ables said.

THE NEXT EVENING on the plaza in front of the abandoned church, the men met to discuss the mine and the temple. They sat on the ground in a circle, with the elders positioned at the center. Settling the mine issue was now urgent, given what had happened. Most villagers were grateful for the National Defense Agency's help, but many wanted life to get back to normal.

"Roberto and I," Tomas said, "have asked Senora Rodriguez to make an offer about the mining at the temple."

Rodriguez stood up at the edge of the group. She spoke in Spanish. "Thank you, Tomas. The first priority of the American consortium is the protection and conservation of the temple. Consequently, we will mine carefully, which means more slowly, so you won't make as much money as quickly as you might from some other group. You can appoint a committee to inspect our work to make sure we're being careful enough. And you'll be able to claim all the crystals you want for religious or cultural purposes. So far as the financial arrangements, we'll do the mining and split the profit fifty-fifty. You'll be able to examine the financial records. Also, we'll use our connections to get the best prices on any technologies you want to install in the village, such as solar panels, satellite connections, water treatment, etcetera. Any questions?"

A man raised his hand.

"Yes?"

"What will happen when Chile and Bolivia reach an agreement on the mine? Will they take it over?"

"I don't know. The US State Department is working with them to reach a solution. We hope it will include our continued participation, but that will be for them to decide."

"So they could nationalize the mine?"

"I don't know. Sorry I don't have a better answer."

Another man raised his hand. "What about jobs?"

"There will be some mining jobs. But most new jobs will be a result of projects you develop with your mining profits. If you build an electrical system, for example, you'll need workers to maintain it. Or satellite internet. Or water purification. It's really all about how many modern conveniences you want."

Another man cut in. "But if the mine is nationalized, the government could take all the profit."

"Maybe. I don't know what could happen in that situation." She looked over the crowd. "Any other questions for me?"

No one spoke.

"Thank you, Senora Rodriguez," Tomas said. "Now, if you will excuse us, we need to discuss our options."

"Of course." Rodriguez started down the cross street toward the path up the hill to the temple compound.

"All right," Tomas said. "Before the Muslims and Lysenko's people were fighting over the mine, some of us thought maybe we could just go on as we always had, but those days are gone. There is going to be mining."

Most of the men nodded their heads.

Roberto continued. "The Muslims and the Lysenko Group both claimed they would put our concerns first, but they each did what they wanted as soon as they had the chance. The only one who has proven she will do what she says is Senora Rodriguez."

"Thus far," one man said.

"We need to move quickly," Roberto said. "We don't want any more vultures swooping in on us. The Americans can provide the soldiers to protect us and the mine."

"I think we should petition the government for soldiers, not rely on the Americans," another man said.

"But which government? I always thought we were in Chile, but now no one knows," a third man chimed in.

"And what if the government takes over the mine? We'll have no say in the protection of the temple, and we might not be able to keep any of the ore," another man said.

"I don't think we should have too much technology. It will corrupt our way of life," someone said.

"That's a different discussion. When we have money, then we can decide how to use it. Right now, we need to decide about the mining contract," Roberto said. "If we go with the Americans, we can always put a limit on the contract. Five years, perhaps?"

"I agree with Roberto," Tomas said. "I never thought I'd be saying that." He looked through the crowd. "Anyone else?" No one spoke. "So, will we go with the Americans?"

Most of the men nodded their heads.

"Anyone with strong objections?"

No one spoke.

"Well, then. We're going with the Americans on a five-year contract. Roberto and I will inform Senora Rodriguez."

They went up the hill to the temple compound, where they found Rodriguez and KD sitting by a small fire.

"Roberto, Tomas," Rodriguez said, speaking in Spanish, "I didn't expect to see you so soon."

"There was no reason to wait until tomorrow," Tomas said. "The village has decided to go with your offer. Slow mining, inspections, and fifty percent of the profits, but we want to start with a five-year contract."

"I'm sure that will work," Rodriguez replied. They shook hands. "I'll get in touch with the consortium and get the ball rolling. As soon as I have any information, I'll let you know."

"Thank you, Cora," Roberto said.

"Yes," Tomas added, "thank you for everything."

Roberto and Tomas started down the hill.

"How did it work out?" KD asked.

Rodriguez explained.

"Those are very generous terms," KD said.

"The CIA doesn't care how slow the mining is as long as we control the mine. We'll be the only ones with access to the hafnium."

"Then how will you determine the market price for paying the villagers?"

"That's someone else's responsibility."

"So what happens how?"

"I need to get on my sat phone. Let the bosses know where things stand."

ROBERTO WENT BACK to his clay brick house, where Anna was sitting on the steps outside waiting for him.

"Well?" she asked.

"The Americans have the mining contract for five years."

"I checked our bank account. Lysenko deposited money twice. We have enough to go back to the US."

"It's a shame we have to leave," Roberto said.

"Yes, there will be lots of changes here and lots of opportunity for leadership."

"Lots of opportunity to make our village a wonderful place for the next generation."

"But first we have to get help for Little Roberto," Anna said.

"Yes. I pray to God that we'll find doctors in the US who'll have the answers."

"I'm sure we'll find the right doctors in Los Angeles. When do we leave?"

"I know you're in a hurry to go, but let's wait until the mine is actually open. Then we'll know that our people are off to a good start. It's going to take a little while to get the tourist visas anyway."

"Okay, I understand. But I want us to be ready to go as soon as the mine opens. After that, Little Roberto is our only priority."

THE NEXT MORNING, KD and Rodriguez piled Lysenko into a jeep and drove down the switchbacks to the airstrip, where a small turboprop plane sat on the runway. They drove right up to the plane, where two burly men wearing hiking clothes climbed down the stairs. "You Agent Rodriguez?" the nearest man asked.

"Yep."

He showed his CIA ID and then nodded toward Lysenko. "Is this our cargo?"

"He's all yours, gentlemen."

He pulled Lysenko out of the back seat. "We'll take the handcuffs off after we're in the air, Mr. Lysenko."

Lysenko looked from the man to KD and Rodriguez and back again. "Where are they taking me?"

Rodriguez smiled. "Not to the US."

The CIA agent took Lysenko by the arm. "Watch your step on the stairs."

Rodriguez turned the jeep around and started back down the dirt track to the gravel road up the mountain.

"Think keeping him alive is worth the trouble?" KD asked.

"Operational details will change as soon as his associates find out he's captured. But he knows a lot of background info about a lot of bad players. That's the information we're looking for."

"Will he be able to negotiate his release if his info is good enough?"

"A reptile like him? Not a chance."

WHEN THEY GOT BACK to the temple compound, KD went to her tent, found her satellite phone, and sat down on her cot. She input a number she'd memorized a long time ago.

"Yeah?"

"How you doing, Blunt?"

"I was wondering when you'd call. Got home from Walter Reed yesterday. They hit me with some intravenous antibiotics. I start physical therapy in four weeks. I'll be good to go before you know it."

"That's great, Blunt. Still going to make that dance recital?"

"I'll be sitting in the front. How are things with you?"

"It's all been gravy since you left. I'm just supervising security until it all settles down."

"Good deal."

"Give my best to your family."

"You bet. Have you talked to Frank?"

"Can't break silence while you're on a job, Blunt. You know that."

"But you called me."

"You were wounded. That's different. I've got a good spot with the NDA. I'm not going to put it at risk by bending the rules."

"I hear you."

"We'll talk when I get back."

16

Over the next few days, KD, Rodriguez, and the strike team reinforced the perimeter around the temple compound and used the drone to surveil the hills around Agua Dulce to warn of any attack. Rodriguez moved back to her cabin and spent her days in the village, checking up on villagers and continuing to build relationships.

On the fourth day, two mining engineers and a fresh strike team arrived in trucks on the main road and the village held a ceremony for the signing of the contract.

George Ramos, the chief engineer, met with the village mining committee to select the site for the permanent mine buildings and the new road up to the mine. Heavy equipment arrived the next day.

A month later, exploratory mining started, and within the week, Chile and Bolivia reached an agreement on the mine. For the first five years, the villagers would get fifty percent of the profit, and Chile and Bolivia would split the other fifty percent. The Americans would do the mining and buy the ore. The temple antechamber would be protected by cutting a new shaft to the mine face from outside the temple. With the agreement set, miners and security personnel began arriving en masse.

"It's fair," Tomas said.

"Fair enough," Roberto replied. "You'll need to move quickly with village improvements."

"We'll miss your advice."

"We'll be back just a soon as we've solved Little Roberto's developmental problems."

"I hope that's soon, for his sake and for ours."

MEANWHILE, Patrick Colbert, standing in the dark in an empty apartment in Arlington, Virginia, pulled back the drapes on the sliding glass door to the balcony and looked across the street into Jerry Davis's apartment. Blaze had their concerns about Davis. He thought he was indispensable, untouchable, that he could make a deal with the FBI, and no one could do anything about it. Colbert studied Davis's apartment through a rifle scope. The light was on, but he wasn't home yet.

He had to do this job for free. Blaze had called him and told him that Davis could identify him in Kalish's killing, that he was under pressure from the authorities, that Blaze would provide the materials, but they considered this problem to be partly his fault. Cheap bastards. He sat on the carpet and drank coffee from a thermos.

Getting into the US had been troublesome. He couldn't chance coming through customs, so he came in via a gravel road from Ontario, Canada, into New York, driving across inside the Iroquois Indian reservation, and then crossing a farm field to get to the SUV that Blaze had left for him. From there he'd stopped at independent motels on his way driving south, using an assortment of fake driver's licenses, glasses, and hats until he finally got to this apartment, where a sniper rifle had been left for him.

He set up the tripod at the front of the rifle and then attached the scope. Lying on the carpet in front of the sliding glass door, peering through the scope, his line of sight was excellent. He glanced at his watch. Davis should be home at any time. He got up, opened the balcony door, and lay back down.

A few minutes later, Davis walked across his line of fire. He fired twice, the first bullet catching Davis in the neck and the second catching him in the middle of the back. Davis went down. Colbert got up on his knees, disassembled the rifle, wiped it for fingerprints even though he was wearing throwaway gloves, and put the pieces in a paper shopping bag. Then he stood up, closed the sliding glass door, and left with the shopping bag and a satchel containing his thermos. On his way to the elevator, he dropped the shopping bag and his gloves down the garbage chute.

The SUV that Blaze had supplied was sitting in the visitor parking. He'd wiped it for fingerprints earlier. Even though he was supposed to use it to make his escape, he left it there. Getting rid of him was the next logical thing for them to do, and he wouldn't put it past them trying. He walked over three blocks to the Washington, DC Metro, where he took the orange line out to the East Falls Church metro stop. He'd left a Toyota Rav4 in the commuter parking. It was still there, his suitcase in the back seat.

He was completely on his own now. He'd heard that Lysenko was still alive, but that the CIA had him, so he had to assume that the CIA knew everything about him that Lysenko knew. Between them and Blaze, he couldn't go anywhere he usually went. Smart money would be on taking a vacation until everything settled down—a six-month ocean cruise, perhaps. He could make a decision on the drive down to North Carolina.

BASHIR AND SAAD sat in a Range Rover on a side street in the warehouse district of Ciudad del Este, Paraguay. No one else was within sight. With the windows rolled down they could hear city traffic in the distance. Birds circled in the sky.

Bashir looked in the rearview mirror. "Where are they?"

"They'll be here," Saad replied. "You know how late they are."

"No discipline."

"True, but that's the way we like them."

A police van came around the corner, moving fast, and screeched to a stop in front of a three-story warehouse. Police officers wearing tactical gear rushed out, the first two men carrying a battering ram between them.

"Finally," Bashir said.

The two officers battered down the steel entry door next to the garage-style door. The rest of the officers rushed in. A few shots were fired. Four men, hands cuffed behind them, were led out of the building and put into the police van. Then a police lieutenant walked over to the Range Rover.

"Senior Bashir, the warehouse is yours."

"Thank you. Please give my regards to the chief."

"Yes, sir."

The lieutenant got into the passenger's side of the police van, and the van drove away. Bashir got out his cell phone. "Bring the trucks."

A few minutes later, two tractor-trailer rigs came up the street and stopped next to the warehouse. A man got out of the first truck, went through the battered door into the warehouse, and opened the garage-style door. Then the first tractor-trailer rig backed into the warehouse.

Bashir's phone rang. "Yes."

"The information was good. This place is full of military grade weapons and ammunition."

"Excellent." Bashir ended the call.

He turned to Saad. "Let's go."

Saad pulled away from the curb. "That was Lysenko's last warehouse in the city. He didn't even put up a fight."

"His organization is in tatters. No one has seen him since the Americans took the mine."

"Taking over his assets was a genius move. It made up for the money we lost trying to take the mine. The Caliphate Council will be impressed."

"The council weighs defeats much heavier than successes."

"At least now you won't have to worry about losing your post."

"True. But I'm just as far from Iraq as I was before."

"You'll find an opportunity."

"I hope you're right."

THE NEXT AFTERNOON, Jacques Athos and Jan Kowalski sat in Lysenko's office in Warsaw, Poland. Kowalski hung up the phone. "The jihadis took our last warehouse in Ciudad del Este."

"Nothing we could do. They control the police."

"We're out of South America for now."

"We can still ship from Europe," Athos replied. "We just won't have a stockpile, which really makes no difference since we lost the Caliphate as clients."

"We need to come to some sort of accommodation with the Caliphate Council."

"I'm trying, but right now they blame us and the Blaze Group for losing the mine. And they're the least of our worries anyway with the US, Brits, and Germans digging into our cover businesses."

"Lysenko wouldn't turn on us," Kowalski said.

"You've never been under hard interrogation. You'll eventually tell everything you know if they have time to check out everything you tell them."

"At least we're still strong in eastern Europe and the Middle East."

"That's where we should focus until we know the limits of the damage in the west."

"Which brings us back to the New Caliphate Council."

"If we could find them another shipment of Soviet weapons, that's about the only thing I can think of that might win them over," Athos said.

"What's the name of that Egyptian arms dealer who just got out of prison?"

"You mean Ebrahim Fahmy?"

"Yes. Maybe he knows about a stockpile somewhere."

"He hates Lysenko," Athos said.

"Well, Lysenko isn't here. And Fahmy probably needs money, since he hasn't been working."

"Okay. I'll reach out to him. But I'm not promising anything."

"We've got to try something."

KD AND RODRIGUEZ took a turboprop plane from the smugglers' airstrip. As the plane banked to turn, Rodriguez looked out over the view. "First time I've seen these mountains from above."

KD leaned back in her seat. "You came in by car?"

"Jeep. Thought I'd be here a few weeks—develop relationships, get the mining contract, and go."

"Even our end took a lot longer than that. Chasing down leads in DC, tracking bad guys in Europe, and then running and gunning down here."

"It was the long haul for sure, but we did some good work. Plus the bonus of grabbing Lysenko."

"And putting the New Islamic Caliphate on its back foot."

"What are you going to do when we get home?" Rodriguez asked.

"Sleep. What about you?"

"Going to visit my mom. See if my boyfriend is still available."

"Good luck with that," KD replied.

"Thanks."

They switched to a US Air Force jet on the tarmac of a Chilean military airbase and flew overnight to Joint Base Andrews in Maryland. After they landed, they shouldered their duffel bags and walked out to the parking lot in front of the terminal.

"Great working with you," Rodriguez said.

"Same," KD replied. They shook hands.

"Give Blunt my regards."

"You bet."

Rodriguez got into a black Ford Explorer. KD stood at the curb, waiting for her ride. Her NDA cell phone rang. She looked at the screen. Blunt.

"Hey, Blunt."

"Hey, Doc. Welcome back."

"How did you know I was here? I just got off the plane."

"I've got my nefarious ways."

"Tina."

"Uh-huh."

"You must be almost healed up by now."

"And I've still got two weeks sick leave. Hope I can get my wife to take some personal days. Go to the beach down in South Carolina maybe."

"Isn't your daughter in high school?"

"She'll be okay for a few days. Unless you want to stay at my house and keep an eye out."

"I draw the line at babysitting dogs and teenagers."

"You don't know what you're missing, Doc."

"And I don't want to know."

He chuckled. "Frank could go with you. Work out some those wanting a kid feelings."

"You're cruel, Blunt."

"Just trying to help."

A silver Highlander pulled up in front of her. "I've got to go. Enjoy the beach."

"You bet. See you in the office."

When KD got back to her apartment, she dropped her duffel on the carpet by the door and flipped on the lights. Frank wasn't there. She could hear the hum of the refrigerator. The air conditioning kicked on. She walked through to the bedroom and picked up her personal smartphone. The bed was made. Frank's underwear wasn't lying on the carpet.

She turned on her personal phone. She had a lot of missed calls and texts, most unimportant. One voice mail from Frank from the day after she left.

"*Sweetheart, I know I'm not supposed to say this, but I'm worried about you. I know Blunt's got your back, and I wouldn't be of any use if I was there, but that doesn't help. I hope you're safe and getting the job done. Call me when you get back. Love you.*"

KD sat on the edge of the bed and texted Frank. *Where are you?*

She got up, stripped off her desert camo into the hamper in the closet, and then went into the bathroom and turned on the shower. While she was unbraiding her hair, her phone rang. She smiled. It was Frank.

"Katie, when did you get in?"

"Just now. About to take a shower. Are you in town?"

"I'm down at the Kennedy Space Center. Be back in DC on Friday."

"Have you thought more about if you're going to move up here?"

"I have. I've put out a few feelers."

"I've been thinking too. If you can find a job you like, and you move up here, you can just move in here with me."

"You sure about that?"

"I'm sure."

"I can't wait to see you."

"I can't wait to see you."

"I could change my flight. Fly in Thursday evening."

"It's a date."

"I love you, Katie."

"I love you more."

He ended the call.

She tossed her phone onto the bed and went back into the bathroom and got into the shower. She put her head under the spray and let the water sluice down her body. Maybe she was moving too fast. Maybe his moving in permanently would blow up their relationship. Only time would tell. But it was the correct decision, no matter how it turned out. It was the decision that was correct right now.

FINALLY…

Thanks for reading *The Hidden Mine at Agua Dulce*. If you enjoyed it, please post a short review on a review site of your choice. A few words will do. Honest reviews are the number one way I attract new readers. Thanks so much.

I'd love to hear from you. You can reach me at my website: https://michaelpking.org

ALSO BY MICHAEL P. KING